I0663858

THE

perfect

plan

M. L. PENNOCK

Copyright © 2025 M.L. Pennock
Cover design by 315 Designs

All rights reserved. No part of this book may be reproduced or transmitted in any form or by any means, electronic or mechanical, including photocopying, recording, or by any information storage and retrieval system without the written permission of the author, except where permitted by law.

This book is a work of fiction. Any similarities to real people, living or dead, is purely coincidental. All characters and events in this work are figments of the author's overactive imagination.

Also by M.L. Pennock

To Have series

To Have — Brian and Stella's story
To Hold (To Have #2) — Stephanie and Max's story
To Cherish (To Have #3) — Tommy and Jacelyn's story
Letters from Emily (To Have #4)

Famous in a Small Town series

Foster to Family (Book 1) — Delilah and Fisher's story
The Bakery on Main (Book 2) — Maggie and Maverick's story

Coming soon …

Love Notes and Line Drives (Famous in a Small Town, Book 3)

Dedication

for the dads who show up

Table of Contents

Chapter 1

ELISE

"You're late again," I say when he answers.

It's the third time I've called him today, but the first time he's bothered to pick up. I stopped leaving messages on his voicemail years ago. He never listens to them anyway.

"Yeah, I'll be right there," he says, his voice groggy. I'm not even sure he's talking to me as I hear something in the background. A female something.

Looking at my watch and knowing he'll never make it here before I leave if he just woke up, I wonder how we ever thought we could work as a couple. That's right. We didn't think we could. I hoped and wished and tried, despite my better judgment.

"I need you to be here for her. She's four, Tanner. You can't keep breaking promises to her," I say as quietly as I can into the telephone receiver. "Eventually she'll understand that you always make promises you won't keep."

Such poor judgment.

"What's that supposed to mean?" he says, throwing attitude my way.

Should I list all the promises he's broken to me over the years, or just the ones he's broken to Avery? I choose neither. This isn't an argument I want to have. It never changes anything. I learned my lesson.

"Nothing. Forget it. Look, I have to get to work. Just pick her up from the restaurant, okay?"

He groans into the phone. It's the noise he makes when he stretches after waking up and I hate that I know that. I don't want to think about him, in bed or otherwise. If it weren't for Avery, we wouldn't even have a connection and I could have left him behind long ago.

"Yup. I'll see you when I get there," he says.

"Tanner?"

"What?" he snaps.

"Please don't been too late. You promised her you'd come this week. It's been more than a month," I say, quietly. He's always made me feel like I ask too much, and it's taken its toll over the years. "You're also behind on your child support. We could really use that money."

"Yeah. I know. I'll hit the ATM on my way," he says.

I hope I can believe him, but I don't hold my breath.

"Thanks. It's just, she needs new shoes and some summer clothes. She's going through a growth spurt and I—"

"Damn, Elise, I said I would bring the money. You don't have to explain it to me," Tanner says, more awake now.

"Okay. Just ... I'll see you in a while," I say before pulling the phone from my ear to end the call.

Turning to my baby girl sitting at the small table in the corner of our equally small dining area, I paint a smile on my face. I try so hard to not let her see what our situation does to me, but some days are more difficult than others. The stress of limited funds is real, but I make it work the best I can.

"Mama, are we going to work today?" she asks, looking up from her piles of Play-Doh. She hasn't missed a thing. Her eyes sparkle and she's always so happy. My little ray of sunshine. My biggest fear is he's someday going to break her spirit and dull her enthusiasm. He has a way of doing that to people.

It's me. I'm people.

Schooling my features so she doesn't see the sadness, I nod and tell her yes, she's going to work with me.

"I be right back. I'm bringin' my color book and snacks," she says, getting down from her chair and running to her bedroom.

The problem with Tanner is he's a good dad when he shows up. That's part of why I keep letting him pull us along. He's the fun dad. The guy who plays on the playground and chases her all over the yard. He's just not consistent. He wasn't consistent as a boyfriend, either, which is why he hasn't had that role in my life since before Avery was born.

Other people have been consistent, though, and they're the ones who keep me going most days, especially when Tanner lets us down.

Aside from my parents, my best friend, Angela, and her brother have been by my side since before Tanner. But when he came into my life, they stuck by me even harder. I was fresh out of school for early childhood education, but still practically a baby myself when we met. Tanner was fun and fascinating, but definitely not the guy I ever thought of settling down with. He certainly wasn't the man I would have chosen to have a baby with, but things happen. Avery was the best thing to come out of our relationship.

"Mama, I'm ready!" Avery yells, running back into the living room dragging a *My Little Pony* backpack behind her.

Her exuberance is infectious, and her personality is fully reflected in her style. In the fifteen minutes she's been out of the room, supposedly getting her things together to leave, she put a fluffy skirt on over her shorts and slipped a headband decorated with puff balls into her hair. Her hot pink rain boots complete the look. She reminds me of a bubblegum machine — she's always super colorful and you never know what flavor you're going to get; you just know it's going to be one hundred percent Avery.

"You're beautiful, my girl. Let me grab the keys and we'll blow this popsicle stand," I say, reaching for her hand.

"We have popsicles? Where they at? Can I have one?" she asks excitedly.

"Aves, it's just a phrase. It means we're leaving. I don't actually have popsicles."

"You should buy some. I think we need them."

"I will add them to the grocery list," I say as we step into the hallway.

I double check I have my purse and phone, Avery has her bag, and then lock the door to our apartment.

Taking her hand in mine again, we step toward the stairs and I say, "Popsicles sound like a really great idea."

*****

Pulling into the parking lot at the restaurant, I see a familiar little sports car.

The relief that washes over me when I see Damian's car isn't out of the norm. Every Friday, like clockwork, he's here when I get to work, sometimes with Avery in tow if Angela is working the same shift as me and can't stay with her. He just expects Tanner to not show up for his daughter, but he won't say that. Instead, he brings his laptop and sits in a secluded corner drinking water and coffee while he works away on his laptop designing fancy buildings and home additions. He says it's because the office at his house is boring and by Friday afternoon he needs a change of scenery.

When Aves isn't with me, he always asks where she is and, if she's at home with his sister he'll go hang out when he's done "working."

I slip into the empty spot right beside his car, making sure I'm not too close. Turning the engine off, I sit for a minute to breathe before getting out and carrying on with our day.

Unlatching Avery from her car seat, I glance around the parking lot. Tanner's car isn't here. I let out a grumpy sigh and hold my hand out for my daughter to take as she climbs from her seat.

"He's not here?" she asks, looking around at the other cars.

"Not yet. He will be," I say. "Maybe he's going to park out front."

"Can I sit with D?" she asks, pointing at his car as we fall in step and begin walking toward the diner's rear entrance.

I look down at her as we cross the parking lot. I shouldn't say yes. My friendship with Damian always ruffled feathers with Tanner. It's never been more than friendship. Even when I've been single, I've worked hard to not be flirty with him ... though it's been difficult as we've gotten older. The more we grow up, the more he's the kind of man I do see myself with. The problem is, he sees me as an extension of his little sister, making me practically family by default.

"You're going to have to ask if you can share his table. He might be working on something and need all the space," I say, my smile not hiding the fact I know Damian would never tell her no. He always makes time for Avery. "Do you think you can ask nicely?"

She tilts her head as I drop her hand and open the door to the diner.

"I think I can," she says.

Great. It's settled then. I can start working and she'll sit with Damian. I can't afford to lose tips because I'm parenting more than I'm waitressing. Fridays and Saturdays are always our busiest nights and when the specials are just right, I always make a good amount extra from the people I wait on. With this being a second job for me to help make ends meet and be able to put some away in my savings, I don't rely on the tips as much as others do. But, when Tanner waffles on paying his child support, that extra really helps us keep fresh fruit in the apartment.

Avery doesn't even wait for me once I open the door for her. She walks into the restaurant and then takes off at a run toward the back where she knows Damian sits every week, sometimes actually working but usually pretending to be busy until I arrive. I take my time following her, stopping first at the counter to drop my purse and grab a pitcher of water. She's in good hands, so I can take my time before checking on her.

"You're here. Good," Angela says, a bit harried as if we're getting slammed and the kitchen can't keep up. "I was a little worried."

I glance around quickly and notice not a lot going on, but it's not uncommon for her to be concerned if I'm not early. I grew up with the mentality that to be on time you should be ten minutes early and she's well aware of that. When I walk in at my start time, she knows something is up.

"I am. I'm sorry I'm late. I would have texted you guys if I knew I'd be behind," I say without looking up as I write down the evening's specials. Without pretense, I say, "Tanner."

She groans in response. It's not really worth real words anyway. We've done this song and dance for years.

"Where's Aves?" she asks, crossing her arms and leaning against the counter so we're side-by-side but facing each other. I give her a look that tells her she should know where Avery is. "He's a good guy. I'm glad my surrogate niece has Damian to rely on. He's always been a constant for her."

Part of me just hopes he doesn't get tired of us, because I don't see my situation changing any time soon. Not that I want or need any romantic prospects. I can barely handle myself let alone a new guy.

"I think she's getting to the point where she doesn't even care if her father shows up," I say, unabashedly. "She'd rather hang at home with you or sit here with your brother for hours coloring and playing games with him than go with Tanner. He's so unreliable."

"Yeah, he is. But he's been that way as long as you've known him," Angela says, shrugging. "Has he paid up his back child support?"

"Ha! That would be a miracle," I say, tying my apron around my waist. "I reminded him he's behind again and told him she needs new clothes. He was moody about me telling him his daughter is in need of basic necessities. Annoyed, even. He's supposed to stop for cash on his way to pick her up."

Pushing off the counter, Angela grabs the water pitcher I set beside me and, walking away, says, "We'll see."

I know. It's always a case of "we'll see." For the moment, though, I'm going to stop thinking about it and start working. I'm already ten minutes behind and a table of four just walked in. There's no time to stress about my ex. My daughter is here, she's with a safe person, and that's all that matters right now.

I'm going to survive this with a smile on my face, even if it's fake.

I have to.

For her.

*****

"Have a great night, guys!" I say as a table of three local men get up and walk toward the door. They're regulars and I know enough to not hover or stop by to ask how everything is too frequently. They appreciate it and always show that in their tips.

The oldest of the trio turns back and smiles at me. "Have a good night, young lady. The fish was delicious."

I smile back at him, because the fish fry is always good. It's his go-to meal every week. On the rare occasion he orders something else — and I don't question his choice — he usually tells me whatever it was he ordered wasn't as good as the fish.

I'm three hours into my shift, clearing their table, when my phone starts ringing. With an armful of dishes, I rush to the kitchen and drop everything in a bin for the dishwasher, seeking a semi-private location before pulling it from my apron. Standing outside the back door of the kitchen, I answer.

"Where are you?" I hiss into the receiver.

He's got our conversation playing over the Bluetooth in his car. I can hear other people.

"You aren't coming, are you?"

"Elise! Hey, yeah, something came up," he says, as if something doesn't always come up. "My buddy's band is in town and they asked me to come out with them after the show. This could be huge for me."

"You're such an irresponsible asshole, Tanner."

"That's not necessary. I got the money you asked for," he says.

"You mean the money you owe me for our daughter? I didn't ask for it. I reminded you you're behind on your child support payments for our daughter," I say, hoping that by reiterating the money is for our child reminds his friends what kind of guy he is.

"You're splitting hairs, but yes. I put it in an envelope and slipped it under the door of the apartment," he says. "I'll try to stop by tomorrow to see the baby."

"The baby is four years old," I say. Looking at my watch, I feel the frustration mounting. "Look, I need to get back to work. Text me tomorrow when you're on your way over so I can be sure Avery and I are home."

6

"'Kay, bye!" he says, and hangs up before I have a chance to respond.

Sliding my phone back into my apron, I swallow the anger and put a smile back on my face. Pretending is easier than actually being happy. I haven't been happy about Tanner in a long time. This is nothing new.

Happiness is relative, after all.

M.L. PENNOCK

Chapter 2

DAMIAN

I watch her walk back through the dining room from the kitchen. Her demeanor is different. I know when she's faking, and that definitely is not a real Elise smile.

"D, it's your turn," Avery says.

It's our third game of Go Fish while we wait for her useless father. I assume, judging by Elise's change in body language, he's not coming. Anytime Avery has been here to hang out with me and wait for him in the last few months, he hasn't showed up. I really didn't think tonight would be any different.

I pull a card from the pile between us and add it to my hand.

"Go Fish," I say as her hand is already reaching.

Like a seasoned card player, she lays her final match down. Her mother quietly walks up behind her as Avery prepares to make her demands.

"I win. You owe me chocolate milk," she says. "And gummy worms."

My eyes connect to Elise's and she shakes her head. I knew candy would be out of the question, but maybe she'll make concessions and allow the chocolate milk.

"How about a small chocolate milk and we'll save the candy for next weekend when we aren't so close to bedtime?" I say it to Avery, but glance up at Elise who gives me a thumbs up and a real smile as she walks away, her hips swaying just enough that I need to force myself to look away. It's just the way she walks, she's not exaggerating for my benefit, but it's still hypnotizing. She arrives back at our table within moments, carrying two short glasses of chocolate milk in either hand. "I didn't order this."

She smiles at me again, but it doesn't quite reach her eyes.

"I know. But you earned it. She plays a pretty cutthroat game of Go Fish."

I stand from the booth and come toe-to-toe with her. She's my little sister's best friend and I try to not offend her where her ex is concerned, particularly because he's Avery's father and I don't want to upset her by making her think she's not responsible enough to handle things. But ...

"He's not coming, is he?" I ask, just loudly enough for her to hear me. I don't ever want to run the risk of Avery hearing me talk shit about her father. Elise quickly shakes her head, looking down. I'm a full head taller than her, and I hate when she makes herself smaller. I tip her chin up so I can look in her eyes and when I see the hurt, I instinctively clench my jaw. Relaxing my muscles, I take a breath and ask, "Want me to take her home and get her to bed? You don't need to be worrying about her being here with you until your shift is over. She needs to be in her own space, in her jammies, and sleeping in her bed, not tucked away in a booth at the local diner."

"You wouldn't mind?" she asks, timidly.

It always twists my heart when she thinks she's inconveniencing me.

"Never. I wouldn't offer if I didn't mean it. You know Aves is my favorite short person," I say, ignoring the fleeting thought of drawings on my desk at home that still need to be reviewed. "Well, second favorite short person. What do you say, kid? Want me to take you home and get you ready for bed while Mom finishes work?"

She must have been listening closely to our conversation. She's already packed her game and coloring books into her backpack.

"Ready," she says, slamming her empty chocolate milk glass on the table.

"You need her car seat," Elise says. "It's huge. I don't know if it's going to fit in your tiny car. I don't even know how you fit in that thing."

I try not to, but snicker when she says it's huge. I might be a 32-year-old man, but my brain hasn't fully progressed past eighth grade when it comes to certain words and phrases.

"I could just take your car and you drive mine home," I offer, realizing I'm about to hand over the keys to my Corvette. Smirking, I add, "Then we don't have to be concerned about what will and will not fit."

"Deal," she says, pulling her car keys from the pocket of her apron and holding her other hand out for mine. "Just put the seat back where you found it. Whenever you or your sister drive my car, I get in and feel like a toddler."

I place a quick kiss to her temple and promise to put things back where I found them. Reaching for Avery's hand to help her out of the booth, Elise squats down to talk quietly to her daughter.

"Please be good for Damian. This isn't the way our night was supposed to go," she says, pulling her into a hug. "I'm sorry."

10

"It's okay, Mama. D and me are going to have so much fun. He's going to read me books and let me stay up late. Right, D?" she says, looking up at me with doe eyes that I really do have a difficult time saying no to.

Elise looks at me, too, but she's not playing around and offers me a death glare.

"I think," she begins, pausing for emphasis, "Damian should help you get your pajamas on and then read you three books, snuggle, and turn off the light so you can sleep. It's already past your bedtime. Plus, Daddy might be over tomorrow, and I don't want you to be grumpy from staying up late."

"I never grumpy. You always tell me I'm your sunshine," Avery says, her eyes wide.

"Yes, you are my sunshine. Now go home and go to bed," Elise says, softly kissing Avery on the top of the head as she stands to her full height again. Turning to me, she lets out a sigh. "Let me know what you want from the kitchen before my shift is done and I'll bring home snacks as my thank you. Hopefully she won't give you too many issues about actually going to bed. She's a strong negotiator, so you might want to prepare for a long evening."

She doesn't owe me anything, but I agree to text her my order before midnight and remind her that this isn't my first bedtime routine with her daughter. There have been a few nights when she and Angela have needed to get out and have a night of being adults without responsibility along with the times I've kept Avery when both Elise and Angela are working.

"Ready to rock and roll, kiddo?"

"Ready."

That's all the direction I need to grab my laptop bag, Avery's hand, and head out the door.

*****

Bath. Pajamas. An extra snack. Snuggles and four books instead of three.

By the time I turned her light off, I was having trouble keeping my eyes open. My brain didn't turn off, though. Tonight simply solidified my decision to move forward with my plan to start a family.

Do I have a girlfriend or wife to do that with? No. Are there even any prospects? Again, no. Is that going to stop me? Also no. It might make things a little tricky and trying to explain it to my parents and sister could turn into a disaster. I'll deal with that when I have to and probably not before then.

The biggest reason I'm alone in all this is because the one woman I would consider a prospect, I deemed untouchable. Off limits. It's not that I wouldn't want to create a future with Elise. It's that I don't think the interest is there on her part and I don't want to take any chances of destroying the friendship we've always had by chasing after something that might hurt us in the long run. It's a lot to digest, so I've just pined and hidden my feelings, forever being a great friend and pseudo-uncle for Aves.

Realizing she's finally asleep, I force myself off Avery's bed and shuffle to the door wiping the sleep from my eyes. The exhaustion is almost too much, but sleeping isn't an option. I sit down on the couch in Elise's small living room and pull my laptop out. Trying to get work done is better than watching TV and work is a guarantee to keep myself awake. I cross my arms, staring at the screen trying to figure out the best possible solution for what my client is asking me to do.

It takes less than a minute before I click to one of the other open tabs in my web browser. Surrogacy. Egg donors. There's a lot to digest.

I'm midway through reading an article about choosing a surrogate when I hear Avery fall out of her bed. The unmistakable thud has me tossing my computer on the other end of the couch and hightailing it to her room without bothering to close the screen.

"Hey, Sunshine, why are you on the floor?" I ask when I see her sitting upright beside the bed.

"The blue people were ticklin' me when I was gettin' a milk," she says, staring straight ahead but absolutely not awake. Lifting her arms up toward me I take the hint and pick her up off the plush carpet. Laying her head on my shoulder, she whispers, "I tired."

"Let's get you back to bed then," I say, pulling her blankets back with my free hand. I cradle her in my arms and softly lay her as close to the middle of the mattress as possible in an attempt for her to not fall out of bed should the blue people try to tickle her again. Smiling to myself, I think about the stories my mom used to tell me about the crazy stuff I would say in my sleep.

"Nuggle me," she says as I pull the blankets up around her shoulders.

How much longer is she going to want me to hang out with her or "nuggle" her? I stop that thought train and settle myself down on the edge of her bed. Crossing my feet at the ankles and my arms across my chest, I

12

lay as still as possible. As her breathing regulates and she begins softly snoring, I feel my body relax until I can't deny the need for rest any longer.

Chapter 3

ELISE

It doesn't surprise me that I find Damian curled up on top of the covers beside my daughter when I get home shortly before one in the morning. He's got his arm gently draped over Avery and she's doing the same with him, facing one another as if they sleep this way all the time.

For posterity, I snap a picture and send it to his sister.

Thankfully when Avery was moved from a crib to a bed, I skipped the toddler size and went right for a full-size bed. It makes it easier when I'm sitting with her and reading at bedtime. The few times she's been sick in her short life, I've been able to be right there with her, but not resort to sleeping in the rocking chair or on the floor.

My phone vibrates in my pocket as I reach the kitchen and attempt to begin putting food away.

Ang: They're so cute. He needs to find a girl and make me an aunt.

Me: How is he still single?

*Ang: *shrug* He's too busy with work to date and anyone he's dated in the past I would never want for a sister.*

Me: Maybe he'll find someone after you move. Maybe you're holding him back because he knows how opinionated you are. Lol How's the packing?

I still can't believe my best friend is moving away. I know it isn't technically far — it isn't as if she's moving across the country — but it's not just across town, either. She cut back on her hours at the diner for her last week so she'd have time to get everything into boxes and totes. I'm getting used to the idea of closing on Fridays without her, but it hasn't been easy.

Ang: It's ... going.

Interesting choice of words. She's super organized, so I assume her version of "it's going" is nothing like mine would be. Last time I moved, I attempted to pack each room one-by-one, or at least keep like things together and I still somehow ended up with kitchen utensils with my clothes. At least I could chalk it up to the massive amount of brain fog from being pregnant with Avery. Leaving her father in the middle of it all wasn't helpful either. I just wanted to get my stuff and get out.

15

"I really need to start bringing home healthier food for after work," I say to myself as I open the bag from the diner.

Damian never texted me his order, so I grabbed a couple slices of cheesecake and an order of fries on my way out the door. Winding down after work usually includes mind numbing TV and food, especially when I wait tables on the weekend. I turn on the TV, then set my water bottle and the takeaway container of fries on the coffee table before moving Damian's open laptop from the couch so I don't accidentally knock it off the cushion.

I have never made it a habit of looking through other people's things, especially their computers. When I picked up the laptop, though, my thumb must have swiped against the mousepad. The screen comes back to life and lights up as I bend to set it on the coffee table. My mom brain can't help but see certain words and those words — "Choosing the right surrogate for you" — are big, bold, and right at the top.

My phone buzzes in my pocket again. I put the computer down and close the screen as if I got caught with my hand in the cookie jar right before dinner. If Damian wanted to talk to me about something he would. I will not snoop. We have never had a relationship where I needed to hide things from him, and he hasn't hid things from me either. Has he?

Ang: Most of the non-essential things are in boxes. I'm going to miss Cooperstown, but I'm not going that far, so at least I can leave things at D's house or with my parents. At least I still have time and it isn't like my lease is up tomorrow.

I glance at his computer, chewing on my lip as I contemplate. I will not tell his sister what I saw. That's breaching a level of trust I'm not willing to break with Damian. If she knew he was looking into having a baby with a stranger, she would have told me. I'm not even sure that's what he's thinking about, so I can't get ahead of myself with this. He could have been reading an article that piqued his interest. He's one of those guys who absorbs knowledge like a sponge and knows a plethora of information that's useless to a lot of people.

Me: That's great. I'm glad you're making headway. I'm also glad I still have time with you before you leave.

Ang: I'm only going to Buffalo. It's not that far and it's a nice, scenic drive on the good old New York State Thruway. Lol

At least she's truthful.

Me: Aves and I are going to love coming to visit once you're settled in your new place. K, it's late and you need to sleep. Good night.

Ang: Night. Love you.

Me: Love you, too.

Sitting in the dim light of my living room with nothing else to do but eat my fries alone and watch Bluey, I turn the TV off again and opt for doom scrolling on my phone. It's stupid and I shouldn't ... but I jump down a rabbit hole about surrogacy and why people would choose that as opposed to adopting or even actively seeking a partner to love and start a family with.

My eyes get heavy quickly. The day has been long and reading on a tiny screen always makes it hard for me to stay awake after teaching and following it up with a long diner shift. I'm thankful tomorrow is Saturday. Well, technically, today is Saturday. Either way, I'm thankful for the slow morning we'll get to have.

The leftover fries go in the fridge next to the cheesecake. I plug my phone in on the counter, grab Damian's phone from the table and plug it in beside mine, and then turn off the few lights as I follow the path to the hallway leading to my empty bedroom.

*****

"Shhh, don't wake her up," I hear in my half-awake state.

"But they gonna get cold."

"It's okay. We can make more."

My eyes are closed still, but I'm definitely awake now. I can smell the faint scent of pancakes or waffles. Opening one eye just a little, I see Damian at my doorway. Avery stands next to the bed facing him and that has me scooting across the mattress to pull a squirmy preschooler under the covers with me.

Her squeals of laughter bring a smile to my face. Burying my nose in her hair, I breathe in the smell of her shampoo, and wrap my arms around her in a snug hug.

"Mornin' Mama. D and I made breakfast," she says.

Damian is a really nice guy and tall and handsome. He's got a great career and amazing family. He's won the genetic jackpot, but none of that showed up until after being a lanky, all legs, nerd our entire childhood. His single guy status baffles us all.

17

He's still a nerd.

A hot nerd.

"You did? Then I suppose I should get out of this bed and come eat," I say, placing a kiss to the back of her head. She wiggles free of my grasp and throws the covers off us.

He's leaning against the door, watching the entire interaction with Avery, a crooked smile on his face.

"What?" I question, not masking my smile.

"Nothing," he says, but it's obviously something.

That's when I'm reminded of my Internet sleuthing and all the questions I have that I will not, under any circumstances, ask him because then he'll know I saw what was on his computer.

"Take your time. I'll pour fresh pancakes," he says, reaching up to grab the top of the doorframe. "You still prefer chocolate chip or do you want to try blueberry?"

His stomach is on display, just a sliver of it where his shirt has lifted up and his jeans have sunk low on his hips, and for a moment I forget how to use words.

"Elise? You okay?" he asks, and the look on his face is just more proof he is completely unaware of what he is capable of.

"Fine," I respond, probably too quickly, as I pull my eyes away from his abdomen. "I'm fine. I'll be out in a minute. I'll try the blueberry. Thanks."

We exchange a smile before he walks away and I remind myself, just like I used to when I was fifteen, that he is my best friend's older brother. Covering my face with my extra pillow, I take several deep breaths before pulling myself out of the cocoon of blankets on my bed.

I'm dead wrong when I think the rest of the day will go smoothly after waking up to such beautiful scenery.

"You asked me to grab this when I got here. I wasn't sure if you saw it on the counter when you got home," he says, quietly, when I squint at him with my unspoken question.

Damian hands me the envelope Tanner stuck under the door last night along with a fresh cup of coffee and a small stack of pancakes.

"Nope. I was busy talking to your sister and eating French fries. I never even saw it," I say, sliding my finger under the flap. "Well, that's ... disappointing. Sunshine, what do you want to do today before I have to go to work? The park, a picnic, you choose."

Damian eyes me from across the room. Lifting his coffee mug to his mouth, he raises an eyebrow.

"I don't want to talk about it," I say to him. Turning back to Avery, I say, "We could even do a picnic in the park."

"You look like you want to talk about it," he says.

"Yes! Picnic in the park!" she interrupts without understanding she's interrupting. "Can Damian come with us?"

"I don't want to talk about it with her here," I say, locking eyes with him again. "Damian can come with us if he isn't busy. He's always welcome."

"I'm game. There isn't anything on my schedule for today," he says, sipping his coffee again. "If you're done eating, go wash hands and get clothes out while I talk to Mama."

Without hesitating, Avery climbs out of her chair and runs to the bathroom. He watches her every move until she's out of sight, then turns those deep brown eyes on me and it makes my body temperature rise slightly.

"What happened?"

"Nothing."

"Elise, you and I both know that," he says pointing to the envelope on the table, "was supposed to have money for her. How much did he short you?"

I don't want him to get upset. I don't know why I don't want him to get upset, though, aside from it not being his responsibility to make sure my kid has things she needs. That's mine and her father's job. But most of the time Damian does a better job acting like her parent than Tanner ever did.

"How much?" he persists.

"His back support is like a thousand," I say, because when I get two-fifty a month from him and he repeatedly doesn't pay I tend to stop keeping track in my head. It's all written down in the file in my bedroom, though. Looking at Damian, I see the anger flare in his eyes. I might as well drop the bomb now before he asks again. "He gave me a hundred."

"I'm sorry, what? I couldn't have heard you right."

"No. You did," I say, getting up from my chair and carrying my plate to the sink.

Plugging the drain, I start the hot water and squirt some soap on the stack of breakfast dishes. I barely let the water get foamy before I dive in, scrubbing syrup and blueberry juice from the surfaces.

Damian leans against the counter, next to me but facing me just like Angela does when we talk at work, and crosses his arms.

"Okay, I agree to not murder him because there are too many projects on my plate right now and I can't afford to go to jail, but," he says, scrubbing his left hand down his face, "will you at least let me have a conversation with him?"

"You don't have to be my protector, D. I'm not a little kid anymore," I say defensively, but refuse to look at him. Someone has to do the dishes around here. Plus, it keeps me from showing him how close to tears I am.

Crossing his arms again, I can feel the heat of his gaze on me. I just keep scrubbing the plate in my hand.

"You're right. I don't *have* to, but I will be. I've known you since you were what, eight years old? You're my little sister's best friend. I'm not about to let him walk all over you and hurt Avery in the process," he says. "We've had this conversation before."

With the dishes all washed and in the other side of the sink, I still refuse to look at him as I begin rinsing the suds away and placing the plates and silverware in the drainboard.

"I was seven and you were ten, actually. Also, yes, we have had this talk, and just like every time before I'll figure it out. I try to not plan for that money anyway. At least with the little he gave me last night I'll be able to get her the new shoes she needs and maybe take her to the farmer's market," I say. Finally turning to look at him, I add quietly, "This is the way it always is, Damain. He gets to be the fun dad and then forgets about her for a while, eventually pays a little of what he owes and breaks more promises. It's infuriating, but I'm used to it. Avery is used to it."

"My point is, she shouldn't have to be used to it. Your preschooler knows how to budget her finances better than most people in their thirties, okay?"

I laugh loudly at that, but it's true. Avery has always had an interest in how much things cost and how much spending money she has when we go to the store. When you're a single mom, at least for me as a single mom, it just comes naturally to start talking about getting things on sale and using coupons. Avery is a captive audience. I don't complain about money in front of her. I don't even talk about the child support. She just knows we have a certain amount we can spend and sometimes if we go over that, then the next shopping trip we might have to get less of something.

20

"At least she's learning it now. We both know she won't learn it when she's in school. Do they even teach kids how to balance a physical checkbook these days?"

"No idea," he says, smiling at me. "Love how you changed the subject, though. So, picnic lunch in the park? Is that the plan?"

I glance at my phone. No message from Tanner. No surprise. He's going to be a no-show again.

"Yes. That sounds like the perfect plan," I say.

*****

Avery and I set our sights on making lunch, me showering, and both of us getting dressed while Damian runs back across town to his house.

He's worked hard all these years since high school and, unlike me, has the financial security to own his own home. He's an architect by trade but also a wizard with money. When Angela and I were in junior high, Damian started and successfully ran a lawn mowing business. Since all the teachers at school loved him, he usually did their lawns and they always paid well. Smart kid that he was, he saved every penny that didn't go back into maintenance and upkeep for his mower. By the time he graduated from high school, he'd started investing which turned into him being able to be his own boss within a few years of graduating from college. At 32, I don't think the man has an ounce of debt except maybe a small amount left on the mortgage on his house. The house he designed and built, I might add.

Me on the other hand? Well, no point rehashing what we already know.

"Aves, are you almost ready to go?" I yell as I wander down the hall.

Her bedroom door is closed, which isn't out of the norm when she's playing. I quietly knock and turn the doorknob at the same time.

"Hey, Sunshine. Are you almost ready to go to the park?" I ask. I climb onto her bed and watch her play with the small kitchen set I was able to get her for her birthday last year. "If we leave now, we can get things set up at the park before Damian gets there."

Working together we pick up and put away the toys she's gotten out. I pull her hair up into pig tails, her blonde curls bouncing as she skips down the hall to put her sandals on.

I love springtime in our state. Everything comes to life and reminds me how beautiful it is to live in an area with all four seasons. Since the weather is nice, we choose to walk to the playground instead of driving. Armed with a cooler full of lunches and drinks, and a backpack filled with a spare set of clothes and a hoodie for Avery, my keys and wallet, baby wipes for our hands, and a First Aid kit, I point out the daffodils that are popping up in flower beds we pass. We're busy chatting about the faeries that must live nearby, so I don't notice the car creeping along beside us.

"I heard there was a cutie going for a picnic today," he says, looking right at Avery.

Damian's smile is everything to her. He's a safe space to land when other people let her down and I'm eternally grateful for having found Angela and her family when I was a kid myself.

"I'm not cute," Avery says, defiantly. "I'm beautiful."

"Yeah, you are. Inside and out," he says, pulling to a complete stop. Lifting his eyes to mine, he says, "Do you want me to park and walk back to meet you? I can't put her in the car without a car seat."

I tell him that would be fine. I wouldn't mind the extra company as we walk to the park. It's usually just me and Avery during the week, so on the weekend if Angela or Damian are around and want to spend time with us, it breaks up the monotony of having kid conversations all day.

"Toss the cooler and your backpack in here," he says. I raise my eyebrow at him. "Elise, you're going to hurt yourself carrying all of it to the park. Put the bags in the car and we'll grab them out when we get back to the parking lot."

I opt to not deny his help. Opening the passenger door, I toss everything in and roll my shoulders back.

"Holy cow, I didn't even realize how heavy that was," I say.

"Exactly. Weren't you ever taught that when something is heavy it's okay to put it down?"

I stare at him. This is a double-edged sword and I won't win, no matter which argument I provide about not needing anyone's help.

"I feel like you're not talking about the bags."

"You'd be correct. I'll be back," he says, and pulls away from the curb before I can respond.

It feels like only a few minutes later, and I see him jogging back to meet up with us. He closes the space quickly and comes to a dead stop in front of me, breathing as though he was walking instead of running.

"I would be dying if I had tried running that distance," I say to him and laugh for good measure.

He smiles, then reaches down and picks Avery up, setting her on his shoulders and turning to step in line with me as we start walking again.

"You were athletic in high school. You work out. Why do you think you wouldn't be able to run that quarter mile?"

Without a word, I point at my daughter.

"There are several nights I'm forced to eat chicken nuggets and cheese quesadillas. Plus, I do yoga. I don't run."

"Gotcha."

We walk in comfortable silence the rest of the way to the playground, only stopping when we reach the monkey bars and Avery grabs on. Damian dips down to move her off his shoulders and let her hang. When he turns to poke her belly, she giggles and if I were a stupid person I would think this is what my family should look like. Instead, I have Tanner for an ex and he hasn't taken his daughter to the playground since last spring and it was only because I forced him to.

"What's wrong?" Damian asks, his brows furrowed. "You look sad. What's up?"

"Nothing. Can I borrow your keys? I'll grab things out and get lunch set up."

He hands them over, giving me one last curious look before grabbing Avery around the waist with one arm and tickling her with his free hand. Her laughter lights up my whole soul and I smile as I watch her drop into his arms, then run off to the slide as he chases after her.

It's a solid twenty minutes before they take a break from running around the play equipment and join me at the picnic table. I've already set out the containers of grapes and strawberries, and there's a deep covered container with peanut butter and jelly sandwiches waiting for them.

"Mama, you saw me?" she asks, out of breath.

"I did. I think we should see about getting you into the Olympics."

Damian snickers and I smile and she smiles and, for a moment, it's perfect.

"Thanks for joining us today," I say to Damian as I pop a grape in my mouth. "It means a lot that I have friends who haven't ditched me because I have a kid."

Swallowing his water and twisting the cap back on, he glares at me.

"Do people actually do that?"

Scoffing, I nod.

"Oh yeah, you betcha. Most of the 'friends' I had in college bounced when I found out I was expecting," I say. "I can't believe I never told you that. Then again, I never had a reason to. You and Ang stuck with me, and that's what was important."

He makes a sound as if he's thinking about what I just said and then looks at me again. It's a wordless look. What could he really say that his sister hasn't already said about it? Plus, it's been almost five years of losing friends because I'm a mom now. I'm kind of okay with it. If they were meant to be in our lives, they'd find a way.

Avery finishes half her sandwich, all of her strawberries, and most of her juice box before I can figure out what else to say to him. It feels like he wants me to elaborate, but there isn't anything to add. So, I shrug.

"It is what it is," I say, handing a napkin to Avery. "Wipe hands and face, then you can go back to play."

Tossing the napkin on the table after finishing her task, Avery scoots off the bench and rushes to play with the other kids she was running around with before lunch.

Without looking in my direction, Damian launches into a new conversation with me, starting with a dreaded, "So ..."

"Did you close my laptop last night?" he asks. "I remember setting it down when Avery fell out of bed, but didn't put it to sleep or close it."

I've never seen Damian look nervous. Not like this. On the other hand, I must look like I've seen a ghost because his eyes go wide.

"I swear I didn't see anything," I say quickly.

"You don't lie well, Elise," he says, groaning.

"Okay. I didn't see much. Is that better?"

"It's honest. You didn't say anything to my sister, did you?"

"No. Definitely not. For starters, I have no idea what's going on. Second, I hate the rumor mill. Third, it's your business not hers, and when you're ready to talk to her about it, you will."

He takes a minute to digest the fact I saw something, before thanking me for not sharing with anyone.

"Is that something you've been thinking about for a while, or just one of those things where you read a news article and then searched the Internet for information? Because that's definitely not a thing I would have just looked up for the heck of it," I say.

It all comes out of my mouth in a rush, but I cannot help it. If he's just reading random Internet articles, then there's nothing to be wary of, but that's not the way he reacted. It's something important to him. If this is an avenue he's been thinking about for a while and hasn't said anything to anyone about? That makes me sad. He could have support. He could have encouragement. But he's choosing to do it alone?

"It hasn't been heavy enough to put down. At least not down on someone else's shoulders, you know?" he says, a smirk on his handsome face. "Plus, I haven't decided yet. There's a lot to it, like choosing an egg donor and picking a surrogate. That's a hard one for me. The money is just money, but I'm not sure if I want to have a known surrogate or someone I pick from a database."

He's opened the topic, so I take that as an invitation to proceed with my line of questioning.

"What would possess you to spend thousands of dollars to grow a baby with a stranger?"

"Well ... I'm not getting any younger."

My face must respond before my brain and mouth can because he cracks a sad smile and shrugs before looking back over at Avery where she's playing with her new friends.

"But you aren't elderly, either, Damian. You have plenty of time to find a someone."

"I know I'm not old, but I don't have any prospects, Elise. I've tried dating apps, friends have set me up on blind dates, and it's always the same. They either know I have money and want to take advantage of that or they're just looking for a good time," he says. "I'm tired of waiting for Miss Right, you know? I'm smart, financially stable, have a lot of love to give, and want to start a family. Is that so wrong? I'm already connected with an IVF doctor who would handle the actual baby making. I just need the eggs and the surrogate."

I maneuver myself out of my side of the picnic table and walk around to sit beside him. Leaning back against the table, I take a moment to look at my daughter. How different would my life be without her? How empty?

Who am I to tell someone else they shouldn't have a child just because they're single and a guy? No one. I'm no one.

"Not wrong," I say quietly. "How do you think your family will react?"

We both know his sister would be ecstatic to have a niece or nephew. His parents might be more difficult to get on board.

"They're going to have trouble wrapping their brains around a stranger carrying your baby that was created with the DNA of another stranger," I say. Nonchalantly adding, "Science is pretty amazing."

Seeing his smile when I mention science and getting to watch his excitement about the prospect of being a dad is something I could get used to. As a parent, I know it's not always easy. Damian has seen the toughest parts of my parenting journey and he still wants to do this, as opposed to other people's problems being natural birth control for him. Plus, his stance is that he would be helping someone else with their money situation and that's been a big part of his decision-making process when it comes to finding a human incubator — who would be best suited for carrying his baby and could benefit from the funds.

Our conversation gets cut short when Avery runs over and grabs Damian by the hand, dragging him away to push her on the swing. It's exactly the time alone with my thoughts that I do not need.

I wouldn't mind being a little more financially stable. Surrogacy isn't something that ever would have crossed my mind. My pregnancy and delivery with Avery were pretty textbook, even if she did come early, which I know isn't always the norm and for some women it's a total anomaly. But ... what if he wouldn't have to rely on a stranger whose habits he doesn't actually know?

Chapter 4

DAMIAN

"Nah, we just took Aves to the park and had a picnic. I'm glad I was able to go," I say, unpacking the groceries.

"Did you actually make them walk home?"

There's no way Elise said it like that when she talked to Ang, so I'm just going to assume she's attempting to make me feel guilty. It's not going to work.

"I don't have a car seat for Avery. I couldn't drive them home, Angela. Before you even put that thought into words, it doesn't matter that it's only a mile up the road. Her mother would have killed me if I'd tried."

I just need to go out and buy a car seat for Avery. It would be easier. That way we could do cool stuff together when she's with me and I wouldn't have to swap vehicles with Elise every time. She wouldn't be able to ride in the Corvette, but at least I've got other options. My sister thought I was ridiculous when I bought the Yukon, but it comes in handy. Architectural drawings and tools fit without a problem, so I can absolutely add a full-size car seat … and there will be plenty of room for an infant seat when the time comes. I should just start driving that more instead of using the fun car, then I wouldn't have to worry about issues like this.

"Plus, I walked home with them," I add as an afterthought. I don't need my sister thinking I just let them walk home and I drove past them on my way back across town. I know I can be kind of a jerk sometimes, but I will never intentionally be an asshole to people I care about. "After we got everything inside and they got settled, I went back for my car so I could get groceries. It's not a big deal."

She laughs.

"You're so domesticated," Angela says.

"I'm not a cat," I say.

"No, but you are pussy-whipped and it is showing."

I stop, my arm holding the milk in midair inside the fridge.

"What do you even mean by that? Why is that even a thing you would say?"

"You have always bent over backward for Elise. I'm surprised you haven't had to have spinal surgery at this point," she says. I finish setting the milk down and close the refrigerator. "Now, Avery has you wrapped around her finger. I love it. I love seeing you in your element with them, but doesn't it make you sad sometimes that you haven't found someone of your own to have that with? There are so many awesome women out there and you're always shoved away working or playing the cool uncle to our friend's daughter."

I should tell her. Maybe I should start talking to my sister about my plans for starting a family of my own.

But not now. I can't talk to her about it now. There are still way too many details up in the air.

"Look, I am more than willing to date. I'm just not willing to sell my soul to find someone," I say. "What if I found someone and she just doesn't want me? Maybe I'm just broken and not worthy of finding someone who actually wants to love me for me? I'm kind of a nerd and not everyone likes nerdy guys."

"You're the least broken of all of us, Damian," she says quietly. "Maybe that's why I worry about you not having someone. If you can't find happiness, what hope does that give the rest of us?"

*****

I've spent the rest of the day attempting to ignore my conversation with Angela. The last thing I really want is her getting in my head. What I would like to do instead is play the Punnett square game with some genetics and decide on an egg to turn into an infant. Figuring out a surrogate might end up being the easiest part of this whole process when I originally thought it was going to be the hardest.

My choices are narrowed down to three donors. Our ethnic backgrounds are comparable, but trying to decide between blue, brown, and hazel, or blonde, brunette, and red is tripping me up. Does it really matter what color eyes and hair my baby has? I mean, I guess I would prefer something similar to my own, but once my DNA is added, it's a crapshoot. I would like a healthy baby at the end of this. That's my goal.

28

My phone buzzes on the coffee table. I ignore it. It buzzes again, somehow sounding more persistent. Still, I ignore it as I continue scrolling the donor website.

When the vibrations start coming in earnest, I pick it up and see Elise's name.

"Hey, what's up?" I answer the call. Leaning back into the chair, I don't move my computer from my lap and while waiting for her to respond, I click to another open tab with information for the IVF clinic I'm going through. The doctor's office I'm using and the egg donor site he's connected with has been open for years and they're a trusted organization. I could have found somewhere closer, but this office is in New York City and their reputation precedes them. I'd prefer to go with the best when it's something as important as this.

"So ..." she begins. Clearing her throat, she starts again, "So, I was doing some research. About the thing we talked about at the park."

We didn't talk about much outside of Avery and ... oh.

"You have?"

She's got my full attention. Elise is not the kind of person who researches topics unless they really interest her. That's how she got into early childhood education and ended up getting her degree in it. She loves children, but it was so much more than that. She wanted to know about the emotional and social development of children because it bothered her that so many kids don't have the support needed in order to grow and be successful. The restaurant job is just for extra cash to make ends meet because education doesn't always pay well. I don't want to say she can't afford her life, but it's been hard. I help where I can when she lets me, but it isn't often she allows me to pay for more than my share of anything. She's too proud for handouts.

"What piqued your interest? You don't just look things up for fun," I say, adding a laugh at the end to ease any tension she might be feeling. Hopefully, I don't make this awkward for her.

"I don't want you to have a stranger grow your baby," she blurts out. Her voice is shaky when she adds, "Choose me."

Forget about me making it awkward. My mouth opens as her words hit my brain and I close it immediately, swallowing hard. Overcome with emotion, I'm not sure how to react.

"Choose you?" I ask, carefully testing the waters. "That's a big ask, Elise. I don't know if I can ask you to do that."

"You aren't asking. You wouldn't ask. You worry about me too much to ask me to carry a baby for you. Damian, this morning you worried about me too much to ask me to carry a picnic basket on a walk," she says, a breathy laugh following her words. "I'm not asking you to ask me. I'm telling you, if you are sure this is the route you want to take, I would be honored if you chose me."

I'm floored. I know how I want to respond, but I don't know how to get the words out. There are so many things to consider — her health, doctor's appointments, working and being on her feet all the time. Then there's Avery. How would Aves react to her mom being pregnant? Would she be okay knowing the baby wouldn't be her sibling or even living with them? And then there's the fact we'd also be dealing with Tanner and how he might react.

"This changes everything," I say, the thoughts running wild through my mind. "Maybe we should get together to have this conversation?"

"I have to work tonight. Angela is coming to stay with Avery since it's going to be one of her last weekends here before the move. Can we plan brunch? Tomorrow?"

"My place."

It's not a suggestion. I just put the finishing touches on the swing set I designed and built for the side yard and I want Avery to see it. I've kept it a secret and most of my free time has gone to working on it, so it's going to blow her little kid mind when she sees it.

"Text me what I can bring," she says. "Ang just got here so I'm going to let you go. We'll talk more tomorrow."

I want to end the call with an "I love you," because she's one of my closest friends and I do love her, but right now it feels like so much more than love for her. It's straight up adoration and amazement.

"Have a good visit with Angela. I'll see you in the morning," I say instead.

She's offering to sacrifice her body for me to start a family and that is absolutely the most admirable thing I think anyone ever could do for me.

"Don't forget to let me know if I can bring anything. See you tomorrow," she says and then the line goes dead.

I'm not sure how long I sit there, staring at the black television screen hanging on the wall in front of me, before I look at my phone again. She had texted me prior to calling and I hadn't noticed the messages until I hung up from our call.

Elise: Hey, I need to talk to you. Unless you're busy, then it can wait.

Elise: Never mind, I'm just going to call you before I lose my nerve.

I smile at my phone. Suddenly, hair color and eye color are the least of my concerns.

Chapter 5

ELISE

Excusing myself to the bathroom, I let Angela and Avery get down to business making their dinner while I finish getting ready for work. Staring at myself in the mirror, I pull my hair up into a ponytail and then wrap it around into a bun. Eyeliner, mascara, a little lip tint and I'm good to go. This part of my day isn't for anyone but me. It makes me feel pretty and if I can't be pretty for me, no one else deserves it either.

Blowing out a breath after I finish my makeup, I replay the conversation with Damian in my head. Again. I've gone back over everything I said a dozen times. I cut it extremely close calling him when I knew his sister was on her way over here, but I just couldn't not talk to him. This might seem like a snap decision, but it isn't. I would do anything to make sure he is happy, and being a dad? That's something I know he's always wanted. It's something we all know he'd be amazing at. I don't care if he's going about it in an unconventional way.

Lost in thought, I leave the bathroom and go to my room, grab a sweater in case it gets cool out tonight, and mentally prepare for the next several hours of refilling coffee and taking orders.

"Daddy!" I hear her exclaim as I walk down the hallway from my bedroom.

"Tanner? What are you doing here?" I ask, coming into the living room.

Hiding my irritation isn't my strong suit, so I don't even attempt it. He's been around long enough to know what my work schedule is. The fact he showed up right before I need to leave is just plain inconsiderate on his part.

Angela and I lock eyes, and all it takes is one look to know this isn't okay. She's planned her entire evening with Avery. This might be the last time Aves gets to spend time with her for months and I'm not going to let Tanner ruin it for her.

"What? I'm not allowed to come see my kid?" he asks, setting Avery down and patting the top of her head as if dismissing her. "I told you I'd stop by today."

"And I told you to text or call me before stopping over. It's called courtesy and now I'm on my way out," I say, even though I have a little time to spare. "It's not a good time."

He pulls his bottom lip in between his teeth and gives me a once over. A smile that used to make me feel special graces his face.

"I see that."

"Ew. You're such a creep," Angela says from the kitchen. "Why are you here? Unannounced?"

"Look, I forgot to call, but I'm here now. I just want to spend a little time with Avery and then I have to bounce," he says, glancing at his phone. His fingers fly across the screen as he sends someone a message. "They're waiting for me, but I have a half hour."

Angela and I exchange a look.

"That's generous of you. You aren't planning to take her tonight?" I ask, hopeful. It's technically his weekend still. It sounds like he has something going on, though, and I need confirmation.

Looking up at me from where he's sat himself on the floor, he takes a sip of pretend tea from a small purple teacup. Fun dad showed up.

"Um, no. I'm not even going back to my place tonight," he says, brushing his hand up the back of his shaved head. It's a tell, and it says he's about to share with me something I don't need or want to know. "The band met a group of girls last night, so we're hanging with them if you know what I mean."

"I wish I didn't," I say, making a disgusted face. "Watch how you talk in front of my daughter, would you?"

"Are they nice girls, Daddy?"

Tanner's eyes bounce between me and Avery and I wish the floor would just swallow him up and take him away.

"Sorry," he says to me before directing his attention to her. "They seem like nice people, Avery."

She lifts her little pink teapot and pours him more to drink — I hope he chokes — and lets him know she's happy they are nice people. The entire interaction is weird and I hate it for her.

"Can I meet the nice girls, Daddy?"

"Not today, Avery," he says, agitated that our four-year-old won't let it go.

I let them play and help Angela in the kitchen. I need to walk away before my mouth comments something my brain doesn't filter first. As much as I hate him, and will do anything to be away from him, I don't want to say something I would regret saying in front of Avery. I hear an alarm ring and realize he set a timer for how long he would spend with our kid. I bite my tongue. It's only been fifteen minutes.

"I'm out of here. Aves, thanks for the tea," he says at the door. I hadn't realized he even got up from the floor.

Avery jumps up to go give him a hug and I wish I had been smarter about who I thought I loved half a decade ago.

He's distracted by her, wrapped around his leg in a hug, so I ask about the envelope. I don't hit the high notes until Avery has let go and run down to her bedroom to keep playing.

"You're really behind on your child support and owe almost twelve hundred dollars. I'd like, before you leave here today, for you to explain to me how you can afford to go out but not give money to support the child you willingly helped bring into this world," I say, keeping my voice low and my tone direct. It's what Ang and Damian call my 'angry teacher' voice. When Tanner looks at me, he knows I'm not only pissed, but ready to play hardball. This isn't the Elise he dealt with on the phone yesterday. To prove the point, I add, "I want what you owe us by the end of the week or I call my attorney to see what we need to do to start the process of garnering wages."

This tactic has worked before, but I don't know how much longer I can threaten to call the lawyer and not follow through. I shouldn't be put in this position just because I want to provide for my daughter.

"You're scary when you're mad." He leverages a nervous smile.

"You haven't seen me mad, Tanner. She deserves better than what you're giving her, monetarily and emotionally," I say. "Do better for her or stop altogether. It's up to you."

"Got it. I'll get what I owe you this week," he says, forlornly, as he places his hand on the doorknob and prepares to leave. "I'm not very good at this, you know. When it was just us, I knew how to do that. I haven't figured out how to manage life with a kid. I'm not Damian who just steps up for everyone who needs him. I like my freedom."

I'm taken aback, but not as much as Angela.

"Tanner, you didn't even know how to manage when it was just us. That's why it was never going to work and I left before she was even born. You prove that every time we talk."

Without another word he swings the door open and lets himself out.

Turning back to the kitchen I catch the tail end of Angela flipping him the bird as he leaves.

"I can't believe he brought my brother into it," she says. "And if he liked his freedom so much, why didn't he just leave you when you found out you were pregnant with her? Or, I don't know, use a condom?"

I don't have an answer for Angela. I wish I did, but that's just not how this works. I wasn't in a position to not tell him I was pregnant, but I wasn't in a position for him to just up and leave either. Damian and Angela wouldn't have let me fall on my face, but relying on them shouldn't be necessary. It doesn't help that my parents, as great as they are, aren't exactly financially stable either and couldn't do much other than be supportive.

While I was pregnant, Damian was kind enough to help me invest a small inheritance I received from my grandmother instead of leaving it to build the small amount of interest banks are paying on savings accounts. I know how much is in the account and have access to everything, but I've left Damian in charge of the investment. He knows what he's doing and he knows I don't want to touch that money unless my entire life falls apart. The funds are earmarked for Avery — so she can go to college or buy a car or get her first apartment or a downpayment on a first home. I don't touch it. We're watching it grow just like we're watching Avery grow.

"He can have his freedom," I say, finally. "I got the best part of the deal."

*****

There are a lot of days I have stress through the roof with my day job and look forward to having the evening weekend job so I can talk to other adults. I like hearing their stories, from the college kids who are nervously on their first date to the ladies in their 80s out for a late supper after going to see the local community theater production of *Peter Pan*.

Teaching preschoolers year-round is not for the weak. I stick with it because I love it, but there's something to be said for having a break from them and being with other grownups.

"How's that kiddo of yours, Elise?" asks one of my regulars.

"She's doing great. Growing like a weed. She was here with me last night," I say as I refill a coffee cup.

"No babysitter?" he asks.

I smile kindly. I don't like to give out too much info about my personal life if I can help it, even if these people see me every weekend.

"Something like that," I say.

Fortunately, Avery gets to come to preschool with me and her tuition is at a reduced rate. I haven't ever had to worry about daycare, just if I can still cover all the bills after what I have to pay out of pocket for her to be at school. I've been privileged in that respect.

Checking on the rest of my tables, I collect a bill and a stack of plates before going back to the counter to replace the coffee carafe on the burner. All my tables are squared away for the time being and I have five minutes to pee, grab a drink, and check my phone.

Damian: French toast or pancakes?

Me: You did pancakes this morning. Let's make French toast.

I smile at my phone as another message comes through immediately.

Damian: Yeah toast!

Shaking my head at his silliness, my smile grows a little more.

It sucks to know he hasn't found his person so he can make having a family a reality in another way, but that isn't something I want to worry about right this second. Tomorrow, we'll talk about all the things we need to talk about.

French toast and babies and how I fit into all of it.

Maybe this will change fate for him.

The real smile on my face disappears when I hear a commotion coming through the front door and I go into work smile mode. A large group enters and heads straight for my section of booths. I should be happy because it could mean good tips, and I can use all the extra I can get, until I notice who's leading the pack. Then I wish I didn't need the money as much as I really do.

Walking around the end of the counter with a stack of menus, I wait for them to figure out where they're all sitting before I attempt to greet them.

"Elise!" Tanner yells, all smiles as though he's my best friend. He looks me up and down, making the hair rise on the back of my neck. I'm not sure how I ever thought he was 'the one' I could build forever with. Being so near him is making me uncomfortable. When he steps in close to me, I can smell the alcohol on him, which makes me feel sick. Lowering his voice, he moves in even closer. Licking his bottom lip, he says, "I forgot you were working tonight."

"You did not. Please step away from me," I say through gritted teeth. "Sit down and behave."

He lifts his hands as if I just reprimanded him in the harshest way.

"Yes, ma'am." He gives me another smile, his eye flicking to my chest before coming back up to my face. I wish I could leave work and go home. "Friends, this is my baby mama. Baby mama, meet my friends."

Awkward and gross.

"Nope. I'm not playing this game tonight," I say, tossing the menus on the table and turning to him. "First, you stiff me for months on child support and I'm nice enough to not get the court involved. Then you skip every weekend with our daughter for just as many months. Now, you think you're going to come in, choose my section, and be allowed to harass me in front of your friends? No, Tanner. We won't be doing this tonight. Mac!"

I yell for the owner and as soon as his name leaves my mouth, Tanner sits down and stares straight ahead as though he's not going to be a problem for me tonight. He won't be, but it's not because he doesn't want to cause an issue.

"Whatchu need, Lise?" Mac yells from the kitchen doorway. Then his eyes land on Tanner. "We gonna have a problem tonight, Tanner? I'll call your mom if you think you're going to fuck around and upset my staff."

Mac is well aware of the multitude of problems I've had with Tanner since having Avery. He's been there every step of the way right along with Damian and Angela, but he's more of a father presence than a friend. He doesn't take shit from guys like Tanner.

"No, Coach. No problems. We just want to have some burgers and fries and hang out," Tanner says. His friends stare at him like they've never seen someone put in their place before. Maybe they haven't. Maybe it's just that Tanner made them all think he was more important than he really is.

I feel Mac walk up behind me. He's a big guy — six-foot-five, played college football while going to school for business, and the longtime high school coach who never stopped going to the gym — so his presence is large and commanding.

"That's good. I'm glad there aren't going to be issues in my establishment this evening," Mac says, placing his hands on the table and leaning in to make eye contact with Tanner. "The last thing I would like is one of my former best players to get permanently banned from the local diner because he got foolish. That wouldn't be a good look for you."

Tanner nods. His friends continue to stare in disbelief.

"Now, look over your menus, give Elise your order, and tip her well. I hear Avery needs new shoes and, well, shoes are expensive these days," he says, standing to his full height and towering over the table. "Y'all have a good night."

"Have a good night, Coach," Tanner says.

Taking my elbow, Mac gently leads me to the back of the kitchen, away from the noise at the grill and the chatter of the handful of other employees working with us tonight.

"Are you okay?" he asks. It's a completely normal question. One he's asked me every time he's been here and Tanner has come in. Tonight, it feels like too much.

"Not really," I answer honestly, but stare at my shoes. "Thank you for taking care of things for me. He's not a bad guy, he's just … not the guy I thought he was. He's been drinking."

"I know you're kind of a transplant to the area so you didn't know him when he was a kid like I did. We've had this conversation before, but they're rarely the guy you think they are," he says. Placing his hands on my shoulders, Mac encourages me to look at him. "I can put someone else on that table if you need me to."

I can't afford to lose tips.

"No," I say quickly. "I'm an adult. I can handle it. I don't think he's going to be an issue now that he knows you're here tonight. He's always better behaved when you're around."

"If it changes and his group becomes too much, let me know. We'll switch it up and divide the tip between you and whoever takes the table. I'll make it right for you."

Nodding my agreement, I take a deep breath and thank him. I would hug him, but then I might cry. This is no time for runny mascara. When Mac heads back to the office, I step into the walk-in cooler to calm myself down the rest of the way.

He's right. I didn't know Tanner when he was younger. Damian, Angela, and I grew up an hour north of here. Damian moved to the outskirts of Cooperstown after graduating college and when Angela and I were finishing

39

up our college experiences, we opted to move close to him. It's always kind of been me and Angela ... and Damian. But we had career options here, too. It wasn't just because of Damian.

My phone vibrates in my apron.

Damian: Coffee or tea in the morning?

Me: I don't know. Either will be fine.

Damian: That's evasive. I'll make coffee and have water ready in case you decide on tea instead.

Me: That works. Thank you. :)

I've been standing in the cooler way longer than I should and reach for a small bucket of coffee creamers on instinct when the door opens. I don't say anything, just scoot past my coworker and head back out to see if my tables are doing okay and if Tanner's group is ready to order.

Chapter 6

DAMIAN

"I'm surprised Mac didn't toss his ass out of the restaurant," I say when she tells me about last night at work.

Pouring a refill of her coffee, I attempt to wrap my head around how she ended up with a guy like Tanner. He's just not a great person. In the beginning I tried really hard to like him, but he always made me go on the defensive. I know he doesn't like me either, so we never tried to be in each other's presence unless it was something that couldn't be avoided, like Avery's birthday parties.

"He was close. He knows how badly I need the money, though. I'll never be able to afford to move to a nicer area if I can't save the little extra I get from the diner job," she says.

I hate that she's in this situation, but she won't touch the money we've invested until it's an absolute emergency. Elise has that money set aside for Avery and I can't talk her into splitting it so she can at least put some of the interest from it into savings for herself.

"So, speaking of money ..."

I tread gently into the topic of today's brunch. I've got packets of information from the IVF clinic and my attorney. Payment plan and cost and the whole nine yards. Before last night, I thought I was going to have to find someone from a database who I don't know to do this with, so everything I've looked into has been based on that. The way the procedures and money works shouldn't change much if Elise carries the baby for me, but doing this with her means I can be more involved. I think. I don't think she would keep me from being involved. That would be weird considering how involved I was when she was pregnant with Avery, and she's not my baby.

I understand this is a totally different scenario. She might not want me to come to doctor's appointments and ultrasounds and all of that. Would she keep me from coming to those things? I hope not. I don't want her to go through all of those things completely alone ... and it would be my baby, so—

"Earth to Damian," she says.

My eyes snap back to her.

"You were off in your own little world there for a few minutes. Are you okay?"

"Better than okay. I'm just trying to figure out the best way to start this conversation," I say. "I don't want you to think I'm choosing you just because I know you could use the money. It's because I know and trust you."

She nods. Then takes a sip of her coffee and pushes a bite of her French toast around on the plate in front of her.

"I'm glad you trust me. I just ... I don't want you to think I said what I said last night because it would be extra income for me. Growing a baby is hard work, it's exhausting —"

"It's worth every penny you'll be paid," I cut her off.

"And in the end, you'll have a beautiful little person to love and raise, and I'll have a niece or nephew to spoil like you've done to Avery."

We smile at one another. I want this. I want this with her. It takes everything in me to not wrap her up in my arms and smother her with grateful kisses. My mind begins to wander into uncharted territory and I need to snap it back because thinking of kissing Elise is not where my brain needs to be right now.

"So, we're doing this?" I ask.

"We are."

Opening the file folder I set on the counter, I begin thumbing through papers. There is so much information and thankfully my attorney put everything in order for me.

"There's a contract to sign and a physical you need to have done. I don't know how invasive it all is." I swallow hard because this is the first time I've really thought specifically what Elise will endure to get my baby into her.

"Considering what I know just from having Avery, I'm sure I can handle a pelvic exam and the pregnancy part. From what I've read, the doctors will need to put me on medicine to make sure we're hitting my cycle at the best time to transfer the embryo and then we wait a week or two to test and see if it took," she says, proving my point about her need to research things. "The science behind getting pregnant is fucking insane. Like, the timing needs to be pretty perfect for this to work."

We sit quietly as she reads through the information in my folder until she gets to the printouts with the egg donors. Her eyebrows furrow, but I don't want to interrupt her thoughts so I get up and check on Avery.

When I built this house, I wanted to make sure it was big enough to raise a family in. Elise having Aves gave me the excuse to turn what would be a sitting room or library into a small playroom without imposing on one of the three extra bedrooms. I do tend to spoil Avery, so some of her little kid toys have found their way into one of the spare rooms for storage. But, that's because she's getting to the age where we get to play with all the cool toys together so those are taking up space where infant type toys used to be.

Poking my head in, I watch as she sits on the carpet in the middle of the room and works to build with a new set of LEGO I picked up. It's the classic set, so they're simple designs, nothing extravagant with wheels and super tiny parts. From where I am, I can see she's put together an ice cream cone and a unicorn so far. I hope she leaves them together when she's done so we can put them on the shelf in my office or on my desk. They'll go great with the pictures she's drawn me.

Leaving her to continue playing quietly, I open the sliding door on the opposite side of the house and step out on the deck. It overlooks a small lake and I have the best view for clearing my head. I'm leaning on the railing with my coffee mug in one hand when Elise joins me. The perplexed look on her face is the first thing I notice.

"Are you choosing a donor based on non-disclosure or no?"

I'm caught off guard. It's not because she's questioning it as much as how I'm unsure how to answer.

"Will it be a problem if I don't want to know who the donor was?"

"No, but thinking about how DNA and health and all that stuff could affect the future for this baby, I think ... look, it's not my place, but maybe consider choosing someone who opted for being identified in case there's a health issue," she says. "Regardless, she won't be this baby's mother. She's just a source of genetics and genetics are kind of a big deal."

Nodding, I tell her I agree with her. That's why, of the ones I've narrowed my choices down to, all but one chose to have identities disclosed. Plus, as this baby gets older and has questions, I want to be able to have a way to get answers. Each of the donors I've considered have half a dozen eggs available, which means my son or daughter could potentially have five other siblings at some point. I don't want that to be a secret from the little person I create.

"This has been in the works for more than a year, Elise. I've definitely thought of almost everything."

"Good," she says, definitively. Biting the inside of her cheek, her lips purse slightly. "More than a year? And you haven't said anything to anyone but me?"

Leaning back against the railing, I take a good long look at her.

"Yup."

"But, why?"

"Because I trust you with my life and if I can trust you with my life, I can absolutely trust you with the life of my unborn child, whether that's just with the knowledge that I'm going to become a father through surrogacy or you're going to be my surrogate," I say. "I trust you implicitly."

Elise steps forward into my personal bubble, lifts her chin and looks me dead in the eye. I have more to say, though, so I start talking again before she can respond.

"It doesn't matter that you found out differently than I intended. You were always meant to be the first one to know," I say, smiling, though it's a sad smile. "I love my sister and my parents, but Angela is moving away and I don't want this to be a reason for her to stay here. And my parents ... as much as they want to be grandparents and are open to different views, would ask me why I couldn't just find a wife and have a baby the old fashion way. As if I haven't tried."

She nods and shuffles her bare feet.

"But mostly it's because out of everyone I know, you're my best friend, and my kid sister's best friend, and you know me better than anyone."

Her eyes are misty and I know I'm the reason she's ready to cry, so I set my mug on the railing and open my arms wide for her to fall into.

"Thank you," she whispers against my chest. "Thank you for choosing me to give this gift to you. I cannot wait to meet the baby you make."

Chapter 7

ELISE

It's been a whirlwind the last several weeks. We got Angela moved into her apartment in Buffalo. Then Damian and I took Avery to New York City to do the touristy thing — Central Park, a Yankees game, museums, a Broadway show she fell asleep at before intermission.

We used the trip as a recon mission, of sorts, as well. He showed me where the clinic is and we planned out where to stay when we go back for the transfer. Because of the distance, my doctor and the fertility doctor have worked together to make sure I'm taking the correct medications to prepare my body for the transfer. Things are right on track. Everything is going to plan. I think.

"Two? Are you sure?" I ask him.

"If they fertilize two, we have another shot if the first one doesn't take. Or … we can have a second baby in a couple years and it's the same DNA profile. Is that okay?" he asks, as if this isn't his choice alone. I mean, it's my body, but his choice about how many eggs.

I try to hide my smile behind my napkin so as not to draw attention to me. Spending time with his family and my parents for Father's Day maybe isn't the best time for us to have this conversation. There are only so many times he and I can sneak away to discuss something else he's thought of as we get closer to our transfer date before one of them questions our motives.

But my hidden smile isn't a mocking one. It's the way he's referred to a second baby. "We can have" is a lot different than him saying "I can have" and I'm not even sure he realizes what he said.

"It's your decision," I say, taking a sip of my water. Looking at me from across the table, he gives me puppy dog eyes. "D, you don't need my approval for this."

"But I want your thoughts and if you think it's too much, we'll just do one," he says.

"Do one what?" Angela asks from behind her brother. I didn't even see her coming our direction and my surprise is apparent. "Or did I hear something I shouldn't have?"

Damian and I exchange a look; I shrug and he nods. We've talked about when we should let the rest of the family know and, honestly, this is the only time we'll all be together before we go back to the clinic.

"It's time?" he asks me.

"Probably the best time," I say, my voice cracking with extra emotion. Thanks, hormone shots.

Getting up from the picnic table, Damian walks purposely into his house. I watch him through the large windows as he heads toward the kitchen where our mothers tend to congregate and in moments he's coming back to me. Both sets of parents in tow, and Avery on his hip, he opens the sliding door and steps out. He looks more like someone's daddy than I've ever noticed before. He's more of a daddy than my own daughter's father is.

"Are you okay, Elise? What's the matter?" Angela asks. "You guys are acting weird."

I shake my head as Damian brings Avery over to me and sets her on my lap.

"I'm fine," I say, but it's the least convincing I've ever sounded. "You'll see."

Our parents sit down in the other chairs surrounding the table and I can tell they're all confused. Damian has not sat down. Instead, he's taken to pacing the deck and, as he walks past me, I snag the beltloop on his shorts with my pointer finger. He stops and looks down where I've caught him, then his eyes meet mine.

"It's going to be fine," I say, but this time I'm confident, because it really is going to be okay. We're doing this and they're being invited along for the ride. "They're all waiting."

He turns and it's all eyes on us. This weird little family we're becoming is the center of attention.

Damian takes a deep breath and swallows, then reaches for my hand and squeezes it.

"I know you only want what's best for me and want me to be happy. I am happy. I could be happier. You're always asking me when I'm going to settle down and start a family, and as much as I've put myself out there, there really aren't many women interested in a guy with a house on the lake once they realize that guy also has a giant LEGO collection he isn't willing to part with," he says, injecting humor where it's needed. "But that doesn't mean I can't start my family."

He squeezes my hand again and I tighten my grip. Watching our family and their faces as the realization dawns that he's holding my hand and not letting go through this conversation is the amusement I needed this afternoon. They have no idea what's coming next and I am so excited for it.

Angela and I share a glance. She narrows her eyes at me, knowing I've been keeping things from her since she moved. I would feel bad about that, but this was Damian's news to share. I promised him I wouldn't tell her.

"A little more than a year ago, I decided to look into surrogacy and egg donors," he says, a nervous laugh punctuating his words. "There's literally no way to sugarcoat this. Elise has offered to carry a baby for me."

"I'm sorry, you did what?" my dad asks.

I slide Avery off my lap and ask her to go play on the swing set while we talk. She knows what she needs to know, but just in case it doesn't go the way I expect, I'd rather she not be within earshot.

"Maybe it would have been easier to just say we're having a baby, but that would have been weird too because we aren't technically having a baby together," Damian says. His palm is clammy and as I watch his face, small beads of sweat begin to glisten in the sun along his hairline.

I've never seen Damian nervous. Not like this anyway.

"Here's the deal," I say, drawing the attention to me. "Damian wants a family and I'm going to provide the body for a baby to grow. We're already in the process, have done the doctors' visits and physicals and everything else. What you need to understand is, Damian is going to make an amazing daddy and he needs the support from both of our families."

Silence. Utter silence from them and all I can hear is the water lapping the shore and the leaves rustling from a gentle breeze. His mom looks from him to me and back. She starts and stops what she wants to say, and when she finally gets it out, it goes pretty much exactly as I suspected it would.

"I'm going to be a grandma?" she asks, eyes wide. Reaching for Damian's dad's arm, she slips her hand into the crook of his elbow and wraps her other arm around it, holding on as her excitement takes hold. "We're going to be grandparents!"

Looking up at Damian, I squeeze his hand once more before letting go and mouthing, "I told you." Earlier today we discussed how this could go.

He predicted it would not go well, there would be anger and tears and everyone would leave and want nothing to do with him or the baby. I, on the other hand, said his mom was going to flip out in the best way and his dad is going to be happy in his own way. We both determined Angela was going to feel confused and hurt because we kept this from her, but that she ultimately will be happy for her brother.

I glance over at Damian's mom and mine talking about how exciting it is to be grandparents and all the fun things they can do once the baby is here. The baby isn't even a collection of cells at this point, but the fact they are so excited means more than anything.

"When are you due?" Angela says quietly from the seat next to me.

"Don't know yet."

"What do you mean you don't know yet?"

"Well, the only thing I'm growing right now is a cushy place for an embryo to land, but there's no baby yet," I say, counting the days in my head.

Once Damian gives his semen sample on Friday, there should be something growing within a few hours.

"If all goes as planned, we go for our transfer late next week," I say. I hear the waver in my voice and I see the moment she notices it, too. As excited as I am, I'm still nervous. Pregnancy comes with so many unknowns.

"How did all of this happen? I didn't know you were even thinking about surrogacy, or that my brother was considering it," she says. "I've missed a lot since deciding to move."

"Hardly. This all came about at the beginning of last month," I say, counting back on my fingers. When Damian and I really started planning it fell almost perfectly with my cycles. My body has taken to the prep as if it was yearning for another baby. "Long story short? I saw something he had open on his laptop and it became a conversation and then I might have said 'choose me' and he did and here we are. He chose two eggs and the doctors we're working with plan to fertilize both on Friday."

Her eyes go wide.

"You're going to have twins?" she says excitedly, but her volume remains quiet so as not to draw attention.

Shaking my head, I feel my heart begin racing and a nervous laugh escape.

"No. Absolutely not. He's fertilizing two, saving one for another time and transferring one," I say. "Unless the first one doesn't work and we start over right away."

She looks slightly crestfallen to learn there won't be two embryos transferred, but I'm okay with her disappointment.

My dad has slowly made his way over to the side of the table where I'm sitting and I don't miss the concerned look on his face. I can feel the worry radiating off him. He was the same way when I found out I was pregnant with Avery. That's what makes him the best kind of grandfather. He gives a shit.

"What's Aves think about all of this?" he asks, sitting in the chair on my other side ignoring the fact I was in a conversation with Angela. As if she knows this talk is going to be a rough one, Angela gets up, places her hand on my shoulder, gives it a gentle squeeze, and walks away to talk to her brother. "Is she going to understand you can't keep the baby?"

Straight to the point. But he's the one I expect that from.

"We've talked to her about it a little bit. She understands I'm going to have a baby but that baby will be more like her cousin and not a brother or sister," I say. Not that my daughter even knows what a cousin is at this point since she doesn't have any her age and doesn't really care when I talk about mine. "It'll become easier to understand for her as things progress."

"Yeah, I get that."

Dad and I sit together in the quiet for a few minutes. I know he wants to say more, but he's struggling to figure out how to approach it. The way he pulls his lip in and looks out over the water is telling — he has big thoughts and is trying to find a way to say it. What he actually says shocks me.

"I'm surprised he's going this route and you two didn't just get together. Probably would have been easier to make a baby that way. Cheaper, too."

Choking on my water, I cough to clear my airway.

"Did you actually just tell me I should have had sex with my best friend's brother to give him a baby?"

"I'm your father. I would never say it like that. Plus, I've thought for years the two of you would end up together," he says. "He looks out for you, but I think there's always been something more."

I know my dad hates Tanner. He never liked him when we were together and now that he's turned into a fairly absent father who only comes around when it's convenient for him, Dad's opinion of him is not good at all. But it never crossed my mind he thought Damian and I would date.

"I don't think Damian thinks of me that way," I say. "I'm just his friend and I'm doing this for him because I love him and am willing to sacrifice myself and my body for a year to see him be happy. Plus, baby snuggles."

"He compensating you?" He leans his elbows on the table and steeples his fingers under his chin. He won't look at me, but I know it's because he's concerned. He doesn't like to let me see that side of him too often.

"He is. I don't want you to worry, Dad. It's all been reviewed by attorneys and is legit. The money will help when funds are tighter than normal," I say. "Let's face it, if I'm able to start putting a little aside because of this it's just a bonus. Is the money important? Of course it is. Am I doing it for the money specifically?"

"I hope not."

"No. Absolutely not," I say, and a feeling of déjà vu washes over me.

Dad releases a sigh and drops his forehead to his hands.

"You always were a handful growing up," he says. I smile. I know for a fact I was a complete angel. Most of the time. "You doing this for a good friend doesn't even surprise me. Just do me a favor. Keep your mother and me in the loop so we know how things are progressing."

As if I wouldn't.

"Are you kidding me? You two are probably going to be my first phone call when that pregnancy test turns positive," I say, smacking him gently on the arm. Getting serious with him, I add, "At least this time it's planned, you know? And the baby will have an amazing father instead of someone who only shows up when he wants to."

*****

"That seemed to go well, right? They all sounded excited and happy," Damian says as we clean up his kitchen after our picnic has ended.

Angela is on her way back to Buffalo and once she left, my parents gave hugs and kisses and excused themselves to head home as well. Damian's parents stuck around a bit longer, helping bring the rest of the food in from the table outside and spending a little extra time with Avery. They've loved her like their own grandchild since finding out I was pregnant. I guess it makes up for where her father's side of the family lacks.

50

"I think your parents are overwhelmed with all the information we threw at them." We didn't intentionally overshare about the process, but they asked questions and we answered them. "But excited and happy sounds much better, and I think once they process everything that's exactly where they're going to land."

"And what about you?"

"What what about me?" I ask placing condiments in the fridge. Turning to face him, Damian hands me a steaming mug of coffee, light on the milk and sugar. I lean against the fridge and inhale the aroma while contemplating his question. "Am I happy and excited?"

I've cut back from the several cups I would normally have to one in the morning and one in the evening, so I savor every sip. Lifting the mug to my lips my eyes flutter closed, but I feel him watching me. It doesn't matter. I'm going to enjoy this. When I pull the drink away from my mouth and open my eyes, all I see is him watching me.

He blinks away whatever I thought I saw in his eyes, smirks, and says, "I was thinking more about how overwhelmed you must be, but if you're also happy and excited I'll take it."

"I'm all of it. But now that my parents know and Angela and your parents know, it eases some of the stress of who might take Avery when we go down for the transfer since we'll be there a couple days," I say.

"You don't think Tanner is going to cause any issues?"

"With?"

"All of it. You being pregnant, especially you being pregnant with my baby. Avery staying with your parents or mine. There's a lot happening and I'm afraid he's going to give you a problem once he finds out, that's all."

I've thought through every possible scenario where this pregnancy is concerned, including how it's going to affect Aves and how her father will react. I always come back to "my body, my choice" because I do worry that Tanner is going to be problematic, but he's only part of my life because of Avery. What I choose to do with my body isn't up to him.

"Maybe we should call a family meeting with Tanner. The three of us sit down and tell him about the surrogacy. I don't think it's going to change anything for him. We'd be doing this as a courtesy to him," I say.

Taking a handful of steps from the refrigerator to the counter, I wiggle my way up onto one of the bar height stools so I'm a little taller for this conversation. Damian continues to watch me without a word and I wish I could be in his brain.

"A courtesy," he says, coming to the opposite side of the counter. Leaning down onto his elbows, he looks directly into my eyes. The hormones I'm on are already messing with my libido, but the way he's looking at me? It kicks all the tingling up a notch. He nods, completely unaware of what's happening to my body when he looks at me like that. "Okay. Let's call a family meeting."

"Can we do it tonight?" I ask.

He smirks. I close my eyes when I realize what I said versus what I meant and how he tends to turn those kinds of phrases around. With all the things I'm feeling, though, I don't want to go drawing more attention than necessary.

"Can we have a family meeting tonight?" I restate and clarify.

He chuckles and I refuse to open my eyes. I can feel the heat rising in my cheeks. My ears are burning.

"You are such a child," I say, covering my face as I begin laughing.

"I make life fun for you," he says. "Without me, you'd have work and Avery. I bring you joy."

I hear the seriousness in his voice, and slowly pull my hands away from my face. His tone lacks the essence of sarcasm I'm used to when he's joking around, and his eyes convey how serious he is when I look at them.

Glancing down at my hands as they cup my half drank mug of coffee, I wait a beat before answering because my throat feels so full of emotion that I'm afraid if I don't wait nothing will come out.

"You do," I say quietly. "You make me happy without trying."

Chapter 8

DAMIAN

We drove separately back to Elise's apartment since I'll have to go home after this "family meeting." Tanner was supposed to be coming over to see Avery tonight for Father's Day anyway, so it's the best time to hold this conversation. He's not going to be happy to see me, but I'm also not going to leave telling him our plan entirely up to Elise. If he reacts poorly, I don't want her alone with him. He's never hurt her, that I'm aware of, he's just a douchebag.

A douchebag I've been picking up the pieces after for years at this point.

"What time is he going to be here?"

"I asked again and he said seven. So maybe he can help get Avery to bed and then we'll talk?"

That sounds reasonable enough. It's almost time, so I put myself to work in her tiny kitchen. I know the Sunday routine is usually Avery's bath, then Elise gives her an hour to wind down and play quietly while she preps fruit and veggies for the week, and once that's done it's a book to read and bed. Avery's already been through the bath and is busy with her dolls in the bedroom when I decide to make myself at home.

I pull strawberries and grapes from the fridge and as if on cue, there's a knock at the door.

"Holy shit he's actually on time," Elise says, leaving me in the kitchen while she answers the door.

Staying quiet, I begin the job I've given myself. I don't want to interrupt his time with Avery, regardless of my opinion of him as a person. With my back turned, I hear Elise open the door and let him in. There's small talk, and I know she hates small talk, so she tells him Avery is in her room and goes to get her.

My heart twists a little when I hear Avery exclaim at seeing him in the apartment. I'm not sure the last time she actually saw him aside from video chats.

"You okay in here?" Elise asks me, coming to stand beside me at the counter.

"Me? Yeah, I'm doing great. Strawberries are almost done. Want to help with the grapes?"

We work together silently as she allows her daughter the time with her dad and my respect for her grows immensely. After how poorly Tanner has acted and how crappy a father he's been, I'm proud of her for being able to still attempt to coparent with him. It can't be easy. So, while I think of all the ways she's amazed me over all the years I've known her, Elise makes herself busy. Together we quietly listen as Tanner is forced to play dolls with his daughter, each smiling conspiratorially at the other when Avery tells him he's playing wrong or to make one of the dolls say a certain thing.

The room gets quiet and we hear wrapping paper tear. Avery made him the typical gifty things for the father person in her life while at school — she goes daily with Elise and I know she's thankful for having the option to bring Aves with her — but I won't share with Tanner that I got one, too. She brought it this morning when we were setting up for the picnic.

"I love it. It's awesome, Avery! You did a fantastic job," he says, plying her with compliments. He's not lying, though, because for a four-year-old she really did put her whole heart into the handprint fish she made this year. "I'll hang it in my office."

"Office?" Elise whispers next to me.

"Did he get a new job?"

"Are you almost ready to brush teeth and have a book? You've got school tomorrow and need your rest," Tanner says, and that gets our attention. "I've got to talk to mom about some stuff."

Avery gets up from her spot on the living room floor and heads to the bathroom. Tanner comes to the kitchen, where he notices me for the first time.

"Damian. I didn't realize you were here. You didn't even say hello," he says, and his feigned maturity surprises me. He puts on a good show for people who don't know him, but I do know him. He's not the guy I ever would have chosen for Elise. Not by a long shot.

"Sorry, man, I was trying to help get things ready for the week so Elise didn't have to worry about them," I say, wiping my hand on a towel and then draping it over my shoulder. I hold my right hand out and he grips it tighter than necessary, but I don't feel like getting into a pissing match with him. "I'll go check on Avery so you two can talk."

Elise touches my arm as I step between them to go to Avery, and when I turn my head to look at her, the unspoken message is her begging me not to be gone long. It's exactly this moment that I stop thinking and lean into her, kissing the top of her head.

"It'll be fine. I'll be right back," I say, leaving the room in search of Avery.

As I make my way down the hall, I hear him ask, "What's that about?" I don't hear her response, but I hear his tone loud and clear. I don't need to hear what she says to know she's mentally preparing herself for what's to come.

"Hey, Sunshine. You ready for bed?" I ask at the bathroom door. There's toothpaste foam all around the outside of her mouth and a huge grin on her face.

"A-most," she says before spitting into the sink. "Daddy's going to read me a book. I have one all picked out and after the book he's going to 'nuggle me and then I'll go to sleep."

She always has a plan worked out. She likes her routine, and if that's what works for her that's what works for us. At least she's flexible when she needs to be.

I help her finish at the sink and then brush through her hair one more time to make sure she doesn't have any tangles before we go out to get Tanner. I'm not sure what to think when we walk in on a conversation that truly doesn't include me and definitely shouldn't have Avery's input.

"So, you're moving to Texas? To be a band promoter?" Elise says.

The look on her face is all I need. She's horrified that he won't take into consideration he's going to be almost two thousand miles away from their daughter.

"Not just a band promoter. Yes, the band is going to be there, but I'll be working for the record label. This isn't a gig that pays under the table, Elise. It's a steady paycheck," he yells. "I thought you would be happy because it means more money for you. Fuck, I can't do anything right."

I see the first tear fall and can't keep my lips from moving.

"That's great, Tanner. I think Elise is just upset because it's kind of sudden, isn't it?"

"Stay out of it," he says to me.

Reaching down I pick Avery up and do exactly what he asked.

"Come on, let's pick out an extra book. I'll read to you while Mommy finishes her conversation," I say, hating that she's witnessed his behavior. I know it's not the worst she could hear or see, but it's not the best. He never gives her his best.

"But I want Daddy to read to me, too."

"I know. He will. Give them a few minutes."

I tuck her in and climb onto the other side of the bed and begin to read. All the while, I'm hoping Tanner gets his emotions under control before coming in to say goodnight.

$$*****$$

Two books later and I can't hear anything going on in the other room from Avery's bedroom. When Tanner comes to the door, Avery is half asleep, so I switch spots with him and refuse to exchange a single word until after I've checked on Elise.

"He's leaving tomorrow, Damian. That asshole hasn't said a thing to me about this and now he's leaving?" she says. Disgust laces each word, but there's also hurt. "I can't believe he'd think I care more about him being on time with his support payments than I would about him spending actual time with her."

"How long has this been in the works?"

"A week." She swipes at the tears staining her cheeks. "One week and he's going to just up and move away from her. I don't get it."

I don't either, but I don't have the words she needs to be comforted. She doesn't need words from me as she attempts to process what's happening. She needs action. I pull her into me and hold her until she relaxes against my body.

"Should we still tell him?" I ask.

"There's no reason not to. He doesn't get a say in what I'm doing with my body. No one does but me."

She hasn't left my arms yet when Tanner comes back into the living room and says, "See? You don't even need me around. You have him."

Her arms tense as she fists the back of my shirt. This isn't going to go well. Elise is a nice person, but she doesn't mess around when it comes to people talking to her in a way that makes her feel diminutive. She's five-foot-five but try to belittle her and she acts six-two and bulletproof.

"Yes, Tanner," she says, sweetly, pulling out of my arms. "I do have him. He's been a constant in Avery's life. He's been here when you won't be. I won't apologize for my friendship with Damian when I've known him for more than twenty years. You don't get to say who is in my life and who isn't. You don't. That's not your role."

"You've always wanted him instead of me."

He's intentionally trying to get me involved and when I try to say something to defend myself, she steps protectively in front of me.

"This isn't a competition and you need to stop treating it like it is. When you walked in here tonight like Dad of the Year, I thought maybe you were changing the way you were coming at your relationship with Avery. You just prove me wrong all the time," she says. "Stop worrying about the child support you never intended to pay on time or otherwise. I'll figure it out on my own."

Bulletproof. Stupid to let him off the hook for what he owes his daughter, but she's just hardheaded enough to not back down when she's decided something. He knows she's shutting him out and there's nothing he can do about it.

"Can I at least still see her when I'm in town? Call to talk to her?" he asks. There's a small amount of fear in his voice as if Elise would actually tell him he can't see Avery.

"I can be a bitch, but I'm not inept. I won't attempt to take her away from you, Tanner, and give you something to fight me on. I never have. It's never been a thought," she says. "If you don't make time for her, that's on you."

The three of us stand there, me as an onlooker as he attempts to find a comeback.

"I was really hoping my news would go over better than this," he says, running his hands through his hair. "I thought me making actual money would make you happy. I'm sorry if I ruined your evening."

"You didn't ruin it. I needed to talk to you about something going on with me anyway and it has nothing to do with your relationship with Avery. That's why Damian is here," she says.

I guess we're just going for it. Elise walks over to the small dining table and pulls out two chairs and sits in a third without another word. Then she waits for us to join her. Once we're all seated, she begins. I watch him for reactions. His face is a range of emotions from shocked to sad.

"You can't just find your own girl and make a baby like we did? You need to do it in a lab?" he scoffs.

I close my eyes and take a deep breath so I don't strangle him.

My answer is a simple "yes" and I'll leave it at that. He doesn't deserve my explanation.

"Well, I guess we're all just making big, life-changing decisions lately," he says, leaning back in his chair and crossing his arms. "What do you want from me? Congratulations?"

"Nope. We're telling you as a courtesy because of Avery. The last thing I wanted or needed was to share the joy of creating life for someone else, her telling you I was having a baby, and then you shitting all over the experience," Elise says, her voice laden with spice and attitude.

I love how she keeps checking his behavior with her teacher voice. But still, he struggles to understand how it all will work, and we attempt to keep the science out of it while explaining the important parts.

"So, you're going to carry a baby ... for him. Give birth. Then just hand it over for him to raise?"

"Yes."

"And you think you aren't going to get attached to this kid? How can you just give him your baby at the end of this?" Tanner asks, a look of disbelief on his face.

"It won't be my baby. He's using a donor egg. I'm sure I'll get attached on some level, but not because it's my baby."

His brain finally catches up and I see when it all clicks and the gears start turning. Elise never said she was attracted to him because he's intelligent, so I assume it's because he was a jock with a pretty face and a musician.

"Wow. Okay. Here I thought my news was going to be earth shattering."

The way his mood has shifted back and forth since he walked through the door is reason enough for me to see how he and Elise never would have worked out in the long term.

"Well, yours was and if you don't stay in contact with her there's going to be fallout I have to handle. Don't make me have to handle your business, Tanner. I want Avery to have a good childhood and so far, it has been," Elise says, standing from her spot at the table.

We both know she's signaling the end of the conversation and about to have him leave. He reads her body language and stands as well, taking steps toward the door where he slips his shoes on.

"As for my news, she's been part of everything since the conversation began. She knows as much as we need her to and have been able to explain to her on her level," Elise says, and I smile because there have been a lot of conversations where a degree in biology would have come in handy. Avery tends to ask very specific questions. "She might only be four, but she doesn't let me hide much. I'm surprised I've been able to keep my frustration with you as under wraps as I have. Even then, she knows something is up when you break a promise."

"You know, I don't try to break them," he says.

"But you don't try to not break them, and that's the issue," she says, opening the door. "Good night, Tanner. Let us know when you arrive in Austin so Avery can send you some drawings for your new place."

He nods his head, says a quiet good night, and is gone from view before I finish standing from my seat at the table.

I give her a minute to close the door and collect herself before approaching.

"What can I do?"

"Everything you're already doing."

"I feel like I could do more, though."

"You could. But it's not something that could even remotely be a possibility for a few weeks."

She turns and reaches for me, her arms encircling my waist as she places her ear to my chest. As if she's just realizing what she said, I hear her gasp.

"Oh my god, please ignore that last statement."

I laugh. It's deep and throaty and makes her sigh. Unfortunately for us, I can't ignore it. But, I won't bring it up and I won't pressure her for an explanation. I'll take care of things when I get home.

"Ignore what?" I ask with every ounce of sincerity I can muster.

"Good boy."

If I never had a praise kink before, I do now.

Fuck.

M.L. PENNOCK

Chapter 9

ELISE

The last week has been nerve-wracking. If I'm not worrying about tomorrow, I'm worrying about a million other things. Naturally, none of them are things within my control.

"You ready?" he asks, reaching for my bag.

I lift it to his outstretched hand and slide my phone into the pocket of my sundress.

"I'm good to go," I say.

Turning to my mom, I remind her of Avery's school schedule, bedtime routine, and the prepped meals in the fridge. It doesn't matter that I have everything written down on a notepad on the counter. I won't feel like I told her unless I verbally tell her.

Avery has two days of school left this week, but I took today off work since Damian and I are leaving before she gets out for the day today. We aren't seeing her before leaving for the city. I made sure to spend extra time snuggling this morning when I woke her for the day, but it suddenly doesn't feel like enough. Our entire world is about to change and I wish I could give her just a few more minutes.

"I have no idea what I'm doing. I've never had to run a schedule for a child before," Mom says, sarcastically. "Baby girl, we will be just fine. Dad and I have it under control."

"I know you do. I just worry about everything."

She pulls me in for a tight hug.

"Well, for the next five days, I want you to worry about one thing only and that's getting this new bean in place so in two weeks we can celebrate a successful trip to the doctor's," she says quietly in my ear.

I tighten my grip on her. We are so thankful to have the families we do. Damian and I have gotten nothing but support since our announcement almost two weeks ago. Support comes in so many forms these days — the text messages asking how I'm feeling leading up to our appointment tomorrow, the book suggestions and articles about pregnancy as if I haven't done this before, and the late-night phone calls with my best friend who is beside herself excited and nervous.

"I love you, Mom," I whisper back.

"I know. I love you, too. Now … get moving or you're going to get caught in worse traffic than either of you want to deal with."

Damian reaches for my hand and leads me away to the car. Opening the passenger door, he makes sure to help me as I step up into the Yukon. It's the first time I've ridden in it since he bought the massive SUV last winter. We just never drive anywhere together, and when the weather is nice, he always drives the Corvette. I find myself touching the leather seat, the softness calming my nerves as he rounds the front of the truck and makes eye contact with me.

He says something to my mom and she gives him an encouraging smile and a hug before he opens the door to climb in beside me.

"Everything's okay?" I ask. I don't know why; it just feels like I need to make sure he's okay, too. I might be going through all the physical changes, but he's a ball of emotions, too.

"Perfect," he says, turning to look at me. "Everything is going to be great. We'll get there and get settled in the hotel, then find something for dinner. Sound good?"

"Perfect," I repeat, smiling at him. "We've got almost four hours of car time. What music are we listening, to?"

He starts the engine and slowly pulls out of the parking space beside my car before responding.

"You pick. I'm fairly easy to please," he says.

"Are you now? We'll see about that," I say, connecting my phone to his stereo system. "Good luck and odds in your favor and all that. First up, Ed Sheeran."

He groans. But, the joke's on me. From the moment the first notes of *Bad Habits* play through the speakers he sings along like a seasoned car karaoke player.

*****

"Here you go. Two keys for room twelve-seventy-one. Enjoy your stay!" the desk clerk says.

Damian slides the keys off the counter and thanks her. Pulling his suitcase behind him and picking my bag up from where I dropped it next to him, he steps ahead of me in the direction of the elevator bank.

"You only booked one room?" I ask, falling in step beside him.

"It's got two beds and a view of the park," he says, nonchalantly.

I didn't want to cause a scene while we were standing at the check-in counter because I was unaware of the room situation, but now that we're the only ones waiting for the elevator it seems like the best time to bring it up. Not that waiting until we're in the room would change anything. Plus, I don't really want to make a big deal of it. It's not a big deal.

"Are you not okay with that?" he asks.

I stall. It's not that I'm not okay with it … I've just had more feelings lately. A lot of feelings.

"It's fine," I say, unconvincingly.

He side-eyes me and I shift my feet.

"Fine?"

Taking a second to breathe and count down from five, I respond, "Yes. It's going to be fine. This way if I want food you won't have to be bothered from a different room down the hall or on a different floor to get me something. Or, you know, things like that."

As the doors open, I turn to look at his profile and find a smirk situated on his beautiful face. His jawline strikes me as powerful and nothing like the face of the boy I used to know.

"Right. Things like that," he says, nodding. "I never took you for a passenger princess, but this trip is proving me wrong."

With that he steps into the elevator with both bags, then places his hand strategically to keep the door from closing as I stare at him, my mouth agape.

"I'm only a passenger princess with you, apparently. It's never happened with anyone else," I say defiantly, smiling as I step into the car with him. "Then again, no one else has ever treated me like a princess."

Wrapping his arm around my shoulder, Damian pulls me into his side and kisses the top of my head.

"Better get used to it. I'm not about to let you be knocked up with my baby and not treat you like the queen that you are."

Just like that, I'm breathless. The elevator is too small. And he smells so good.

Maybe one room isn't the best idea. Regardless, there's no way anything can or will happen with Damian. As much as I'm attracted to him, and it seems he might be attracted to me, there's a contract and rules to follow with what we're embarking on. I'm not allowed to have sex right away. Not that sex is on the table for the foreseeable future … it's just one of those things I miss about being in a relationship with someone.

"Earth to Elise," he says from outside the elevator.

"Huh?"

He laughs, but he's gentle about it. He doesn't make me feel like I'm a lost puppy, even though I may as well be one.

"We're on our floor. Would you care to join me?"

Stepping into the hallway and closer to him doesn't make my previous thoughts better, especially not as I deeply inhale as I walk toward our room.

"Did you just … smell me?" he asks, following me down the hall.

"No, sir, I did not. I was just taking a deep cleansing breath while thinking about all the amazing things we're doing together this week."

Liar. I'm a liar. I was absolutely trying to smell him again. How did I spend four hours in a car with him and it not affect me? Oh, that's right, because prior to checking into the hotel we were not sharing a room and he was not saying I'm a princess or a queen or whatever and all of those things just sort of —

"Elise? You're doing it again," he says.

I snap out of my reverie and realize he's already opened the door to our room and set the bags inside. He lifts his hand and beckons me to come within, flexing his pointer finger.

"I'm coming."

Oh, I wish, I think to myself. Shaking my head to make the filthy thoughts go away, I remind myself to get my shit together. It's just the hormones making me boy crazy. My body is humming. It's just a physiological response. This is basic biology.

Taking another deep breath, I enter the room and he softly closes the door behind me.

Chapter 10

DAMIAN

I need a cold shower. What the hell is happening?

Trying not to watch as she walks through the hotel room and sets her purse on a chair in the corner, I focus more on unzipping my suitcase and pulling my pants and shirts out to hang in the closet.

"You actually unpack when you stay in a hotel?" she asks from behind me.

I can't look at her. If I do, I might do something I absolutely would not regret but could mess up our futures. Her body is primed for a baby and if there wasn't already one being made and ready to transfer, I would love to put one in her.

The old-fashioned way.

Adjusting my pants and still not looking at her, I step around the end of the bed and go grab the few hangers I need. Thankfully, things haven't progressed to the point of her noticing, but I'm still a little overwhelmed.

Maybe two rooms would have been better.

"Here," she says, standing beside me. She hands me a pair of my jeans as if it's the most normal thing ever.

"Thank you," I say, taking them from her carefully so as to not touch her hand.

She notices. Elise always notices when I'm not acting right, just like I know when things are amiss with her. The problem is, she's never afraid to call it like it is and I just want to keep pretending things are status quo.

"There's something happening," she says softly. "And we can't act on it."

"I'm aware." We haven't looked at one another since walking into the room. If we do, would we break the spell? I can't do this entire long weekend without knowing where her thoughts are, so I take a chance and ask, "But, if we did, would it make you sad?"

I wait, holding my breath, for her to answer.

She hands me a button-down dress shirt and I drape it over the hanger with the jeans.

"No," she says so quietly I'm afraid I didn't hear her correctly.

She's my best friend. She's my little sister's best friend. She's about to be carrying a baby for me because I so desperately want to be a dad. I've never had anyone I love enough to want to make this a reality with and the girl of my teenage dreams offered her whole self so I didn't seek out a stranger to do it. I cannot mess it up.

"Is it just the hormones?" I ask her, solemnly. I'm fearful it is, because I know the meds to get her body ready for this procedure were going to cause extreme highs and extreme lows … but I don't want the attraction we're feeling to be because of drugs and not because she actually feels things for me.

I wait for her to respond. My heart is pounding and I'm not sure what I'm going to do with the information when she does speak, but it might change the trajectory of this entire relationship.

Taking the hanger from my hand and walking it to the closet, she doesn't say anything. It feels like it's a million years before she reappears at the corner of the room. She stands timidly, toying with her fingers as if she's folding a little piece of paper over and over. My eyes slowly take in her entire body, the way she holds herself, the slightly bent knee beneath her sundress, the relaxed shoulders, and when I look in her eyes it takes every ounce of energy I have to not move.

"No."

Our eyes are locked and I don't know the next move.

"Are you hungry?" I ask.

If I know one thing at all, it's that getting out of this room and around other people will make this easier. Or it should. Us not being the only two people in any given space would be smart right now.

She doesn't even realize she does it, but her tongue darts out to wet her bottom lip before she nods.

"What?" she questions.

"I wish you wouldn't do that."

"Do … what?"

"The lip thing."

She reaches up to touch her mouth, wiping away the dampness from her tongue with her thumb.

"Oh," she says as it registers. "Sorry."

"You don't have to apologize. It's just going to take an act of God to make me not want do all the things I want to do with you," I admit.

"It's only a few weeks, right?"

I look at her curiously, one eyebrow lifting as I silently question her meaning.

"A few weeks and then you can do all the things you want to with me," she says, her cheeks turning the slightest shade of pink as she bites her bottom lip.

Before I can respond — or even consider a response — she walks across the room, picks up her purse, and grabs my hand to drag me out the door.

*****

Her hand never leaves mine as we ride to the lobby and leave the hotel. Stepping out the door to explore, we turn left and fall in with the foot traffic on West 59th Street until we come to a little restaurant with tables out front. The hostess seats us at one of the tables for two and fills our water glasses as we begin perusing the menu.

"Everything looks delicious," she says, and I agree with her, though I'm not looking at the menu.

We decide quickly to get two appetizers and two entrees to share. Since she isn't going to be allowed to drink alcohol, we celebrate the beginning of our new adventure together with lemonade and attempt easy conversation.

All things considered, that's the most difficult part.

After stopping and starting multiple times because of close-ended questions on both our parts, I finally ask, "What are you most nervous about for tomorrow?"

"Loaded question, but okay," Elise says. "I'm most nervous my body will say no way and reject the transfer and then we'll have to start all over again. We've only got two shots at this, or it feels that way. When I got pregnant with Avery, none of that was planned and she stuck. What if with all the planning and prepping ... what if this baby chooses to not stick?"

It's a thought I've had, too. We're on the same page about that at least. I've also been thinking about the two eggs sitting across town and how maybe a two-for-one deal might have been better.

"I value your opinion, obviously, so I need to ask you something," I blurt out.

She stops, her water glass in her hand mid-air, and waits for me to continue.

"What if we transferred both tomorrow?"

"Both?" she questions, looking down at her abdomen and setting her glass back on the table without taking a drink. "You realize you're like a full head taller than me, right?"

Cocking my head to the side and looking at her I attempt to understand what she's saying.

"Damian, between your genetics and the information you know about the egg donor, you're creating a mini tall person. What if there's not enough room in there for two to grow?"

She makes a valid point, but, "Skin is meant to stretch," I say.

"Yes, it is, I agree with you there. But, what if I can't deliver both naturally? What if my doctor won't deliver me vaginally? I love you, and I'm one hundred percent on board, but transferring both could be adding an extra risk," she says, calmly. "I'm unsure transferring both now would be a good idea. Plus, that wasn't in the contract and we're scheduled for one. It's a little late to change our minds."

There's always a risk with pregnancy, but she's right. I don't want to put her into a high-risk category in the off chance the first transfer doesn't implant.

"One, then. We'll stick with one," I say.

"Is that okay?" she asks.

"Uh huh, that's perfectly okay." I'm nodding my head as I say it and probably look like a complete fool.

She's watching me with concern and I don't want her to be worried that I'm saying something just to please her. That's not really the kind of guy I am. Do I want to make her happy? Of course. I'm just not going to lie to make it happen.

"In the event this doesn't work the first time, or even if it does work, and I decide to move forward with the other egg, will you be willing to do this again with me?" I ask in a rush.

"Of course. That actually was in the contract," she says without a second thought. "I know we haven't explicitly talked about it, but that's been my plan. I'm not going to tell you I won't carry another baby for you unless the plan becomes drastically unhinged or our life circumstances change."

"How would our life circumstances change?"

She picks up her half of the grilled ham and three cheese sandwich we ordered and takes a bite. Chewing thoughtfully, she takes her time to finish the bite before answering. It feels like she's taking extra time to chew extra thoroughly so she doesn't have to answer.

"What if you meet Mrs. Right while I'm pregnant and you want to have more children with her? What if I meet Mr. Right and he'd rather I not carry another baby for you? What if," she says. Pausing to wipe her lips with her napkin, she mumbles into the fabric something that sounds like, "What if we explore whatever this is and we want to make one of our own?"

I eye her suspiciously and wait for her to look at me, knowing I would love to ask for her to repeat herself. I won't, but that's mostly because asking would be solely for my benefit and do nothing to add to the actual conversation. I'd love to do nothing more than explore this with her if she'll let us.

"All good observations. Maybe we should play it by ear and worry first and foremost about tomorrow's appointment?"

She nods in agreement, but conversation stalls out again.

What are we even doing? Playing with fire, that's what. My sister is going to murder me.

I'm consumed with thoughts about all the ways Angela would berate me for this entire afternoon and decide I will not talk to her about any of it. If Elise talks to her, that's her decision. They've been best friends for most of their lives and I know they talk about pretty much everything.

"How is everything?" the waitress asks. "Can I get you anything else or are you ready for the check?"

Elise and I share a look that clearly says she's full and I'm going to be eating her leftovers.

"We'll take the check, please, and can I get a small box?"

"Sure thing. Take your time," she says, setting the folio down with the bill tucked inside.

"Can we walk and do some sightseeing after this?" Elise asks as I slide my credit card in the folio without looking at the bill. "I'm definitely not built to live here, but I can appreciate it for what it is."

"I was thinking we'd walk over to the park. I've never been to the carousel at Central Park, so who better to experience it with than you?"

A touch of sadness reaches her eyes for a moment. Though I can't be certain, I feel it's probably because Avery is at home and she loves going to the park to play.

"We'll bring Avery again another time. This weekend is for us," I say, handing the check to the waitress when she returns with a takeout box.

Once the bill is paid and the food packed, I stand from the table and reach my hand out for Elise to take. It's just becoming second nature to have her close to me. When we go home at the end of this weekend it's going to be difficult to leave her at her apartment and not have her near.

Chapter 11

ELISE

Thursday. It's Thursday.

Transfer day is finally here and I'm not well rested or hydrated enough or not nervous. Sleep didn't come easy knowing Damian was in the other bed. The only thing separating us was a nightstand and some carpeting. He looks like he slept poorly as well, but I don't want to bring attention to it. Not here.

I'm still deep in thought when a nurse opens the waiting room door and I'm called back to the procedure room. Damian stands too and asks if I want him to come with me. My heart begins to beat rapidly — it could be from nerves or from him. I'm not sure which.

"Please," I say.

Without a word, he places his hand on the small of my back and ushers me toward the nurse waiting for us. He's respectful and steps out of the room while I change into a gown and get myself up onto the exam table, only coming back in when I tell him it's safe to. Just like at my regular gynecology visits I struggle to relax. I always feel so vulnerable just sitting there. With this being a specialist, you would think they'd want all their patients to feel safe and comfortable. Maybe offer a warm blanket? A fluffy pillow maybe? That would be amazing.

"What are you doing?"

"Huh? Nothing," Damian says after being caught opening cabinets. "I'm not doing anything. Are you ever curious what they keep in these cupboards? Are there snacks hidden somewhere?"

"It's speculums and ultrasound gel, Damian," I say, not hiding my amusement.

I hear the soft tap on the door and then it quietly opens while Damian is still turned with his back to the entrance.

"I'm pretty sure someone must have fruit snacks hiding somewhere in here," he insists, opening another cupboard.

The nurse looks at me with a bemused smile and I shrug.

"No fruit snacks in there, Mr. Nowell, but I can check the breakroom if you'd like," she says.

He turns quickly and smacks his head on the cabinet door. His ears turn bright red as he reaches up to rub the spot he bumped.

"No, thank you. I'm good," he says.

"Well, you just let me know if you change your mind. We don't need any daddies passing out from low sugar around here," she says, chuckling, as she pulls a blood pressure cuff out of a drawer to get a reading from me.

The nurse and I make idle chit-chat about how I'm feeling and what we're doing today. Damian and I opt to have him leave the room during the actual procedure, which wasn't something we had really thought about until asked.

"We're close friends, but I don't think we're quite that close," I say quietly, emphasizing the word "that" and looking at him over the nurse's shoulder as she continues to prep the room.

He smirks and shrugs. The blush creeps up my chest and I feel it bloom into my cheeks. This isn't in the contract.

"Hello, hello! You must be Elise. I'm sorry we haven't had the opportunity to meet until now. Your obstetrician has been so instrumental in this." A kind-eyed man with greying temples enters the exam room and reaches his hand out to me. "Anyway, I'm Dr. Doctor. Do you want to see who we're introducing you to today?"

My jaw opens slightly, and snaps shut.

"Go ahead and say it. Everyone does."

"Doctor doctor?"

"Yes, ma'am. I thought it would be hilarious as a teen to tell my parents I wanted to go to med school so I could really embody the last name. Joke was on me, though. I fell in love with science, which turned into a love of medicine and helping people have babies. So, here we are," he says as if he's had his speech memorized for years at this point.

When he holds up a photograph, I forget why I cared about his name in the first place — it really was just a bit of nosiness on my part — and I reach out to take the picture between my fingers. It's nothing, really. Just a couple bundles of cells, but I know exactly what they are.

"They're beautiful," I say, touching my index finger to the photo. "Damian, look."

I hold the photopaper out as he takes the few steps closer to me.

72

"Your babies."

He's lost. His eyes swim over the images in his hand but he's unable to form words.

"Everything I researched didn't really prepare me for this," he says, his eyes finding mine. Flooded with emotion, he slowly blinks the tears away. "Crazy to think in a half hour one of these little things is going to hopefully be finding a home in there."

He points to my abdomen, and I instinctively touch my belly.

"Are you ready for this?" I question.

He nods his head, then leans in and kisses my cheek.

"Ready."

*****

In less than thirty minutes, the nurse is bringing Damian back into the exam room and he looks every bit the nervous would-be father.

"How'd it go?" he asks, reaching for my hand, but looking at the doctor.

"Textbook. Perfect. Now we wait," he says to Damian. "There's always a chance a single transfer won't take, but medically everything looks great and in two weeks, we'll know if things are progressing. I know it's hard, but be patient and try to not test the minute you leave the office, okay?"

He's joking and it puts me at ease. I was able to relax for the procedure, but it was difficult and I had to do some deep breathing exercises. There was some pinching, which he warned me about, and even though he says things look great, I'm still going to worry until we have a positive pregnancy test in hand and the ultrasounds to back it up.

My brain is going a mile a minute and I miss the end of their conversation, only realizing we're actually done when the doctor reaches out his hand to shake mine.

"It was a pleasure meeting you, Elise. If you have any questions between now and when you see your OB, don't hesitate to call. My card is in the folder with all the post procedure information," the doctor says. Turning to Damian, he extends his hand again. "Have a safe trip back home. Make sure she takes it easy for the next few days."

Damian nods and the two men finish saying their goodbyes before he turns back to me, admiration sparkling in his eyes.

"I'm going to let you get dressed and I'll meet you in the waiting room," Damian says. "We'll go back to the hotel and watch movies for the rest of the day?"

He says it like a question, but it's the best idea I've ever heard and I nod my approval.

"Ice cream," I say as he's about to close the door behind him. He pokes his head back in and lifts his right eyebrow. I elaborate, saying, "I want ice cream if we're doing movies. That's the deal. Movies and ice cream."

"Already with the demands. I didn't think cravings started this soon," he teases, closing the door once more and leaving me to find the underwear I tucked away in my pants.

But as quickly as I felt calm when he came back in the room when the transfer was complete, I feel the panic set in. What if he changes his mind? What if I agreed to carrying this baby and he decides he's not in it for life? What if I'm overreacting and it all works out?

What if all the things he seemed to start feeling for me — things that I've been feeling for him for years and continuously shoved to the deepest parts of me — is just a byproduct of me being his surrogate?

I can't think about that. I can't even think about anything with Damian beyond carrying this baby and keeping him or her safe for the next several months. Love is not an option. Romantic love, that is. I love him as one of my best friends. That's the love we need from each other right now.

Taking another look in the mirror, I fix my hair, touch up my lip gloss, and put on a smile.

"Everything is going to be fine, Elise. It's going to be fine," I say to the scared little girl staring back at me before I blink and she's gone.

Chapter 12

DAMIAN

"Are you sure it's not too early?" I ask through the closed bathroom door.

I've asked her this same question no less than five times since she texted me this morning.

We haven't even reached the two-week mark yet. Elise has been nauseous for three days, though, and it's only been eleven days since the transfer. I think she's coming down with a cold or something from the kids at work, but she swears no one there is sick.

It's also entirely possible she thinks she's feeling sick because she knows we're in the two-week wait and wants to start testing as early as possible.

When I talked to her before she and Avery left for work today, she insisted I come over for dinner tonight and to have a twin pack of pregnancy tests in tow. I stopped at the pharmacy on my way and bought what she needed along with three pints of ice cream.

At this point, I just do what she tells me to. The ice cream is in case we're celebrating or in case we're still waiting.

"Damian, why are you listening to Mommy pee?" Avery says. She snuck up behind me in the hallway. She was supposed to be playing in the living room. "That's weird."

I turn, feeling my cheeks heat at her observation.

"It is weird, right? But we were having a conversation and so we just kept talking when she closed the door and now, here we are," I say kneeling down to her level and motioning to the space between us. "Both of us. You and me. Being weird together."

The door slowly opens behind me and I look up to find Elise smiling at my interaction with Avery.

"Hey, Sunshine. Why don't you go get three spoons out of the kitchen drawer? Damian and I will be there in a minute," she says.

My eyebrows knit together. A shy smile forms on her lips as Avery runs to the kitchen. I feel like the air is sucked from my lungs and I linger a moment longer before standing.

"Are we sad or celebrating?" I ask quietly, reaching for her hands.

75

Without a word she holds two pregnancy tests out in front of her in the emptiness.

"I think we're celebrating, Daddy."

Two faint pink lines. Visible, but not dark. They're right there and I take them in my hand and just … stare at them.

"It worked," I say, hearing the incredulity in my own voice. Lifting my eyes to hers, she has a smile that's as big as her heart and I can't keep myself from pulling her to me. "It really worked. I was so scared it wouldn't work the first time and you'd end up going through all of this again."

I hold her snuggly to me, my heart pounding in my chest while my brain continues to attempt to comprehend what this means. Without thinking, I lift her chin and place a kiss to her lips, one that I deepen the second her lips soften against mine. When a tiny moan escapes her throat, I bite her bottom lip ever so gently and pull away, breathless.

My forehead against hers and my eyes closed, I will my breathing to slow. She's panting softly, her breath warming my shirt and chest, and it's the noise that's going to make me come completely undone for this woman.

"I'm so sorry," I mumble against her hair.

Her body goes rigid and I know I said something she wasn't anticipating.

"Why?" she questions.

Exactly. Why am I sorry?

"I don't know," I respond. "I just got so excited and now … I crossed a line."

Elise doesn't say anything. Her hands find my abdomen and then loop around behind me as she pulls me in for a tighter hug.

"Me, too," she says, and I try to ignore the sadness in her voice. "How about that ice cream? We'll celebrate and get Avery to bed so we can talk about what's next."

What's next are bloodwork to make sure the baby growing hormones are rising, the ultrasound we need to schedule, and her first appointment with her doctor. Going back to Manhattan for all her appointments isn't really an option, so once a heartbeat is confirmed everything will be done locally. Once we get through these first few weeks we can look forward to proceeding, hopefully, as normal with a normal pregnancy and a baby.

My baby.

I'm having a baby.

*****

"I'm not even a full four weeks yet. Are we waiting until after the ultrasound to announce to everyone that it's on like Donkey Kong?"

After she tested — after I overstepped — we agreed to chalk it up to the excitement of the moment. I won't deny feelings for Elise, but I had spent a good number of years burying them because she was with someone else. Before anyone thinks anything different, my feelings also aren't the reason I agreed to her being my surrogate. I trust her and her judgment completely, which is why when she said she crossed a line, too, I was relieved. We're both emotional, but we don't need emotions getting in the way right now.

"I think that might be a good decision. But ..." I say, knowing I sound unsure about waiting.

"But what?"

I shrug because I don't want to make a bigger deal out of it that necessary.

"My sister and both our moms know when you were planning to test. If you don't say something to any of them by Friday, they're going to be blowing up both our phones wanting an answer," I say, standing and walking to her refrigerator. I open the freezer and grab out one of the unopened pints of ice cream, two new spoons from the drawer, and saunter back over to the couch. Elise sits with her legs curled up under her on one end, clutching a pillow to her chest, and I take the other end, stretching my legs out on the cushion between us. "So, I guess either we tell them we got a positive test and want to wait to really celebrate until after the ultrasound or we keep them in suspense and get in trouble with our families because we didn't let them share in our joy."

She reaches her hand out waiting for me to give her a spoon. I take a bite of ice cream first, savoring the mocha cappuccino flavor as I let it melt on my tongue.

"This is so good," I say, pointing to the container with my spoon. "It's too bad you aren't going to be allowed to have a ton of it. Caffeine and all."

I'm still holding her spoon hostage, and as my words register, she drops her arm.

"That's not fair. What flavor is it?"

"Cookieccino?"

77

"There are maybe trace amounts of caffeine in there. There's more caffeine in half a cup of coffee than that entire container," she says, blowing out a breath and causing the hair around her face to flutter. Then she looks at me, a horrified expression on her face. "You aren't making me give up coffee."

I raise an eyebrow, take another bite of ice cream, and try to remain serious. It's not my intention to tell her how to eat, and I made sure that was all spelled out in the contract, but I didn't specifically say anything about coffee.

Before I can respond to her non question, she tosses the pillow on the floor and pushes herself up on her knees so she's straddling my thighs and well within reach of the ice cream and her spoon.

"Hand it over, Damian. You don't tease a girl about ice cream and you certainly don't joke about her coffee," she says, fire in her eyes.

Fuck.

The way she hovers over my legs, the insistence in her eyes at getting her way, is too sexy. I know I must look foolish, my jaw slack and staring up at her. It makes my imagination start working in ways it shouldn't. Like, what if I took another little scoop and offered it to her? From my spoon?

I feel my cock slowly begin to thicken as my brain stops working. As if I'm having an out of body experience, I drag the spoon through the softening ice cream, then slowly lift it to her mouth. Everything slows down as I watch her tongue dart out to wet her bottom lip before she carefully slides it along the underside of the spoon and closes her lips around the bowl as my fingers continue to grasp the handle. Her eyes close on contact. She balances herself with one hand on the back of the couch and places another on my abdomen, just above my belt, and I pray to God I don't come in my pants right here. But then she pulls away from the utensil, and swallows, and licks her lips ... and I know that one "we were just excited" kiss will never be enough.

"So. Fucking. Good," she says. Each word is punctuated and it makes my body need her that much more.

"Are you always like this about ice cream?" I whisper, the spoon still held in midair. "Because I don't know if I can handle you pregnant and ... eating ice cream."

She doesn't even realize what she did. Reality tells me it all happened very quickly, but I swear we've been sitting like this for much longer. She curls her fingers on my stomach and grasps my belt. Unintentionally the tips of her index, middle, and ring fingers graze the tip of my hardened penis as it strains against the fabric of my boxers and I can't stop the sharp intake of breath as the sensation courses through my body.

"Not always," she says, a blush creeping across her cheeks. "May I please have my own spoon now?"

"I don't know if I want to let you have your own," I say, my voice still just a hoarse whisper. "I'm enjoying sharing mine with you."

"Then give me more," she says.

Preparing another scoop, I hold the container closer to me. As she leans in to take the bite, her lips slightly parted, I turn the spoon toward my mouth. Her pupils dilate as I flip the spoon over and suck the ice cream off the metal. Pulling it from my mouth slowly, I watch as her breath quickens, coming out in little exhalations.

"What are you doing to me?" she questions, sliding her hips further up my legs until her core is almost where I want it most.

"The same thing you're doing to me," I say.

Setting the ice cream container and spoons on the coffee table, I never let my eyes leave her. When my hands are free, I place them on her hips and pull her closer to me. The friction from my pants meeting her shorts in all the right places causes her eyes to close and a low moan to escape.

"I love that sound," I say, pushing my fingers beneath the hem of her shirt and feeling the warmth of her silky skin against mine.

She shifts, her knees straddling my abdomen as she pushes all her covered sensitive areas against my hardened ones. The air rushes out of my lungs and my forehead drops to hers. I close my eyes, savoring the moment.

"As much as I love that one?"

I lift my hips to drive myself against her to hear her moan again.

"More," she says, as she reaches for my face and I press up into her again.

My hands on her waist, I push her down onto me as she grinds her core against the contained length of my cock.

Her gasp against my lips is all the motivation I need to continue, but she says again, "More. Please."

I give her what she asks for as she leans into me, angling her pelvis to rub all the best places along the bulge in my jeans. Another moan escapes her lips and I catch it, my tongue darting between to slide along the underside of her upper lip as I pull her hips, dragging her center along the ridge of my zipper.

She nips my bottom lip and releases it as her head falls back exposing the tender flesh of her neck. I sit up farther, my right hand slipping up her back and reaching into her honey brown locks, pulling her head back just a little bit more to give me the access I so desperately need. My lips land gently on the hollow of her neck, and I gasp as she presses herself harder onto my lap before silencing the noise I make by placing my mouth tight against her skin.

"You feel so good against me," she whispers, a low whimper escaping as she completes the sentence.

Her fingers grip the back of my neck, playing with the too long for my liking hairs, before I feel the tips of her fingernails press gently into my skin. I need more of her. I need to see her come undone without me ever touching the hidden parts of her.

My left hand snakes around to the small of her back and as I pull her against me, I lift my hips again. She presses into me, searching for a release, and I drop her hair so she can have full control. Briefly, she opens her eyes and a girl I've never known before looks back at me for a split second before her mouth drops open against the sensation of my body finding the perfect spot on hers and her eyes close again.

It starts as a low moan, seeking an outlet, and as she quickens her movements against me her breath comes out faster until I feel it build in me, too. Watching her find her release is the most gorgeous thing I have ever seen and as her fingernails find my shoulders and dig in, I lift up against her once more and watch her come. Unable to hold my own orgasm back any longer, my cock pulses as I release everything I have on a deep, guttural groan, as she grinds her pelvis into me once more.

I don't touch any other part of her. Our clothes never leave our bodies. And it is the hottest not-sex I have ever fucking had.

Elise collapses against my hard body, her chest heaving deep breaths, as I wrap my arms around her and hold her tightly to me. I kiss the top of her head, stroking my fingers up and down her spine, and feel her hands slip between my back and the end of the couch as she hugs me close.

"This," she exhaustedly mumbles against my shirt, "wasn't in the contract."

Chapter 13

ELISE

Waking up on a Tuesday morning in my bed — alone — is normal.

But I didn't anticipate it being empty today. Not after last night. The thought of what we did, the way my body responded to his, is still fresh on my mind. My body heats again at the memory.

Maybe it was just a dream? When I was pregnant with Avery, my body was in a constant state of arousal when I wasn't throwing up, eating, or sleeping ... and the sleeping parts contained some pretty vivid dreams.

I reach out hoping he's beside me, but before my fingers clasp nothing but the comforter my mind recalls the memory of him carrying me to my bed. My dream theory is suddenly not holding up so well. I can still feel the way he kissed my forehead and the gruff way he said goodnight, as if it was taking everything in him to not climb in next to me. After that, I don't know what happened because I fell into a blissful sleep.

I allow myself to think back through all the little things that transpired yesterday. I tested, and used both sticks just to be sure. Both were positive. Then, the way he kissed me. The way we decided we were both just excited to have a positive result and in the midst of our joy kissing happened. I remember how Damian, Avery, and I celebrated with a little ice cream before Aves went to bed. Then Damian and I talked about when to tell his family, and mine, that it appears the transfer was successful. Then he got out ice cream ...

Not a dream.

This wasn't all in my imagination.

Never in my wildest dreams would I have imagined all of *that*.

I'm not even sure what came over me. It's like my brain turned off and something primal took over.

Damian and I didn't have sex but didn't not have sex. On my couch. After finding out I'm officially growing his baby. His baby. It's so early, still, and I don't want to get my hopes up because I know anything can happen between now and when we go in for the ultrasound to check on everything in there. But I'm hopeful.

As if his little one wants to remind me even more that this is really happening, a wave of nausea hits me and I sit bolt upright, throwing my right foot out of the bed to touch the ground.

"Not a hangover, Elise. This isn't the spins from too much wine," I say to myself.

Lowering my upper body back to the bed after a minute, I push my hair back from my face, then throw my forearm across my eyes, and breathe slowly in through my nose to quell the churning in my abdomen. The clock says it's still only five in the morning, but there's no way I'll be able to go back to sleep after the thought of Damian's hands on my hips last night. Or the way he tugged my hair.

Slowly, I sit up in bed again and see my clothes from yesterday still on my body which is the motivation I need to get in the shower. Smiling to myself, I pick up my phone and send him a text.

Me: Thank you for putting me to bed last night.

It's so early and I don't expect he'll be awake or respond right away. I get myself through a shower, dressed, makeup on, hair done, and start the coffee maker — half caffeinated, but it doesn't really matter because the last couple of days I can hardly make it through the two cups I've been allowing myself. In the last week I've added less and less sugar as it seems to upset my stomach more, and there's trace amounts of milk at this point when I make my cup. I might as well drink it black.

Pouring a commuter mug full to keep it hot for the morning at work, I go in to wake Avery up for school.

"Hey, Sunshine," I whisper against her cheek. "It's time to get up. We need to get ready for work, sweet girl."

"I don't wanna work today," she mumbles, rolling over on her side. I catch just a glimpse of her little smile before her face disappears under the covers. "Can we go to D's house for supper?"

That surprises me. There wasn't any sort of conversation about dinner with Damian tonight.

"I don't know if he's available tonight," I say, my cheeks heating. "I can check with him though."

Shoving the covers off her body, Avery jumps up and wraps her arms around my neck.

"I love going to his house. He has so many toys! And a big swing set I don't have to share with other kids—"

82

"Whoa. That's not how we act," I say, hugging her quickly and then pushing her away from me enough to see her face. "We play nicely and take turns."

"I know, Mommy, but right now there's no one to share with. Not like at school when I don't even get my turn sometimes."

Fair enough. I nod in agreement and remind her once again that being happy about not having anyone to share with maybe isn't the nicest thing because someday she might have to share Damian's toys. I feel foolish, but it's the truth. Someday, she's going to have to share *him*.

My phone dings in the other room and it reminds me there are things to get done, like get the kid dressed and fed and we need to leave.

I kiss her forehead and say, "Pee. Get dressed the best you can. Come out and eat. I'll have fruit and eggs ready by the time you get out to the kitchen."

As she heads to the bathroom, I make my way back to the kitchen. First, a sip of coffee. Next, I pull strawberries and an egg from the fridge. As the pan heats, I wash, dry, and cut the berries, forgetting about my phone again until it makes another noise.

Damian: It was my pleasure. We should talk. Tonight? Dinner at my place. I bought a new LEGO set for Avery.

Did they conspire? I laugh out loud at the message until the part where he said we should talk settles into my head.

Me: Talk? Yes. I agree. But … I need a heads up. Is it bad? Good? Neutral?

Damian: Let's go with neutral. Nothing to worry about. I was just awake last night thinking … things.

Me: Things.

Damian: Yes.

I hear Avery coming down the hall and get back to the stove, quickly scrambling the egg I promised her and plating it with her strawberries. She holds her shirt up to me without a word and I slip it over her head. She hands me socks, and I push them onto her little feet while she sits in a dining chair. Neither of us are huge morning people, so the not talking is normal for us. She gets herself settled in her chair and I place her plate and a small glass of milk in front of her.

Grabbing my phone from the counter and sitting in the chair across from her, I slip my ballet flats on then send one last message for the morning before we make our commute.

Me: See you tonight.

*****

After a hectic day, I sling my bag over one shoulder, pick Avery and her backpack up with the other arm and carry us out the door.

"Elise, wait up!" I hear behind me.

"Huh? What's up?" I respond, turning on my heel and practically dropping my kid. I not so gracefully set her down on the ground and she immediately takes my hand since we're in the parking lot.

"Some of the girls and I were talking about going out for drinks after work tomorrow. You in?"

"Oh, Julia, I can't make it. We've got a pretty busy week, but thank you for the invite!"

No one at work, except my boss who doubles as a somewhat close friend and the ruler of my time off, knows about Operation Grow Damian's Baby and I'm not planning on it becoming common knowledge until we reach the 12-week mark. At the very least. I've even considered just not telling anyone until they start asking questions when I begin showing and it's obvious I'm sporting a baby bump. It's not that I'm afraid anyone is going to share negative thoughts about what I'm doing. I honestly couldn't care less what my coworkers think. I'm more afraid that some of the ladies I work with, the ones with big mouths and even occasionally bigger hearts, are going to try to do all the normal things we'd do for an employee who's expecting — throw a work baby shower and try to get all the information they can out of my four-year-old. Neither of those are things I want happening.

"Maybe next time," Julia says, her smile falling. "I can convince them to skip drinks and go for a bite to eat somewhere so Avery could join us. I know it can be hard to get a sitter sometimes."

"That's so sweet of you. Yes, maybe we can make that work for next time. We really do have a pretty packed week this week, so it's nothing to do with not being able to get a sitter. Promise," I say.

"Awesome. I'll talk to the other girls and see what we can plan for next time then!" She begins walking backwards toward the building. "Have a great night you two! I'll see you tomorrow."

Avery and I say goodbye and wave to her as we make our way to the car. Once buckled, she begins her inquisition.

"What does having a packed week mean?"

"We have a lot going on."

"Do we? What are we doing? Are we going to the park?"

"Um … dinner with Damian tonight," I say.

"Tomorrow?"

"Going to bed early?"

"Mama. Did you lie?" she asks. When I don't immediately answer, she says again, with a stern tone, "Mommy."

Stopped at a red light I look in the rearview mirror and see her arms cross over her chest straps and her little eyebrow raise up until her forehead is a little wrinkly. If she were standing up, she'd probably be tapping her foot on the ground waiting for my answer.

"Not a lie. I'm exhausted and you need your sleep and we have things going on all the time, like Grandma and Grandpa might be coming down this weekend and I don't want you grumpy when they're here."

"I'm not grumpy!" she yells in her defense.

Now it's my turn to raise an eyebrow. Turning in the driver's seat, I stare at her.

"Okay. A little grumpy."

"Thank you," I say, turning back to see the light has turned green.

I accelerate and make my way toward home where I plan to promptly unbutton my pants, take off my bra, and try to figure out how to stay that comfortable when we're at Damian's. I know he's not going to care what I wear, but I just want to be certain, so I send him a text as soon as we walk through the door.

Me: Is this a formal dinner or are sweats acceptable?

I await his response as I lie on my bed with the fan running above me. It's July and I'm thankful I won't be huge pregnant while the weather is the hottest.

Damian: Sweats? Should I turn the air down to frozen tundra levels or are you just looking for something comfortable to wear? This isn't formal. I was thinking grilled cheese and wavy potato chips.

Reading his message, I laugh out loud. He's such a guy.

Then my phone rings.

"I just can't do real pants anymore today. I've been on my feet all day. I'm bloated and other things are already feeling tender," I say as soon as I answer his call.

"Tender?" he asks, concern lacing his voice. "Is everything okay?"

He's never been through all of this from the beginning. Not on an intimate level. Then again, I've only been through it once. Still, I remember this part all too well. The sudden tightness in the waistband of my favorite pants, my breasts being off limits to everyone and everything for months.

"It's fine. Just hormones being hormones. It's happening faster than it did with Avery, though. This wasn't a thing until like eight weeks with her," I say, snickering. Then a sobering thought hits home. "Shit, what if it multiplied?"

"Stop. You convinced me two at once was a bad idea, so don't go thinking that's what's happening now. Maybe it's a boy. If all the things you felt with Avery are stronger this time and happening earlier, maybe it's just because it's a boy. I've read that can be a thing."

I'm quiet. He's quiet. And in the quiet, I feel calm.

"So, I can wear gym shorts and a tank top?" I ask quietly to get us back on topic. "I'm probably going to bring Aves' jammies with us, too, if that's okay."

"Absolutely. Come and be comfortable at home with me," he says.

It's the way he says "home" so easily in reference to me and my daughter that twists my heart a little, especially knowing he wants to have a conversation. A neutral conversation, whatever that involves. We talk quickly about what time to plan for dinner and it gives me about twenty minutes to get Avery ready and leave for Damain's house.

"Is there anything I can bring? Do you need me to pick anything up on the way?" I ask.

From an early age, I was taught to never show up empty-handed when invited to someone's home. It's just the way I was raised.

"I think we're all set. I grabbed groceries today after I met with a client. The farmstand down the road had strawberries still, so I picked up a few quarts," he says. As if he needs to justify why he spent the money, he adds, "I know how much Avery loves them for her lunch and figured what we don't eat tonight you can take home for the two of you."

Has he always been this thoughtful? Have I just ignored it when on the receiving end? Or is it a byproduct of us getting more emotionally attached through all the medical things? I don't want to overthink it. I don't want to worry that he's just being nice because of last night. Not when he said he wants to talk.

"If you think of something you forgot, message me in the next ten minutes so I can have time to stop at the store. I'll get myself and Avery ready and we'll be on our way soon."

"Perfect. See you soon."

We say our goodbyes and I yell for Avery from my bedroom. She climbs up on the mattress beside me and lays down.

"Are you about ready to go to Damian's?"

"I heard you say jammies, so I packed my packpack. I have jammas, fruit snacks, juice box, and my toothbrush," she says.

"Girlfriend, you're not staying the whole night," I say, laughing. "We're going for dinner, but I figured pajamas were a good idea since we won't get back home until bedtime or a little after."

She looks crestfallen, as if I broke her whole heart by saying she wasn't spending the night with her bestie, and I immediately stop laughing.

"Baby, I didn't mean you can't ever spend the night at his house," I say, pulling her to me and snuggling her close to my heart. "But tonight is a school night. We'll talk to Damian and see if there's a weekend you can stay to hang out with him, okay?"

"Promise? Because I love Damian."

You're not the only one, kid, I think to myself.

"He's a super good guy, isn't he?" I say instead. "Let's not leave him waiting too much longer. I'll get changed and then we can leave for dinner. Go grab your sandals. I'll be out in a few minutes."

She pops up and kisses my cheek before sliding off the bed and running from the room to get ready.

I'm barely out of my work clothes when my phone rings. Without looking at the caller ID, I answer.

"Did you think of something you forgot at the store? I'm leaving in five minutes," I say, the phone propped against my ear and held in place with my shoulder as I stumble trying to get my leg through the hole of my gym shorts.

"Nope. Probably should have looked at who was calling first, though," Tanner says in my ear.

Shit.

"Who you going out with tonight?" he asks, but I'm frozen. It's the way he's saying his words. It's the slurring. "Answer me, Elise."

"Tanner, you're drunk."

"I know that. I want to talk to my kid," he says.

I pull a tank over my head and huff loudly.

"Not drunk you're not," I say. "You've had plenty of days to call and talk to Avery and you haven't. Did your guilt catch up to you once the Jack hit rock bottom?"

When Tanner drinks whiskey he's not the guy I thought I loved, and he's definitely not the guy I thought I was having a baby with.

"Don't fucking play with me. You said you weren't going to take her away from me. Let me talk to my kid," he snaps.

"I'll put you on speaker, but the first questionable thing I hear you say and I'm hanging up."

I'm still holding the phone to my ear when I walk out to the living room.

"Mommy, we're going to be late. Let's go!"

I hold my index finger up to tell her wait, pull the phone from my ear, and click the speaker.

"Avery, your father wanted to say hello," I say.

"Hi, Daddy! Mommy and I are going to D's for dinner. He's making grilled cheese and I'm going to play on the swing set and maybe have a sleepover."

And it's that last part that ignites the angry drunk.

"Oh, you are? Well, isn't that just lovely. I'm sure you and Mommy are going to have lots of fun ... having a sleepover at Damian's."

I hear the tone shift; I can practically see the sneer on his face. Avery is too innocent to know. It doesn't matter, though, because I feel my face heat with frustration.

"What did you want to talk to her about, Tanner. We're on a time crunch here and need to leave," I say.

Sliding my feet into my flip flops and picking my purse up off the coffee table, I usher Avery out the door.

"I thought I didn't need a reason to call?"

"You don't, but we have plans and if you don't have anything in particular to talk to her about, maybe she could call you back tomorrow after school."

"Nah. I don't like that plan. So, Avery, do you miss me?"

That's a loaded question if I ever heard one. I hand the phone to Avery as I buckle her into her car seat so she can talk while I get us moving.

"I guess so," she says, timidly. That's not the type of question she's been asked before ... by anyone. "Are you coming home to see me soon?"

"You guess so. That's awesome," he says. I hear him muttering under his breath but don't catch what he says. "Probably not coming home for a while. It sounds like I'm not needed anyway."

I grab the phone back from Avery and close the car door. Taking him off speaker, I suck in a big breath before responding.

"What is the problem, Tanner? You're off living your life and we're living ours. What have we done that you don't approve of now?"

"Why the attitude?"

"You. You are why. You're slurring, you're getting angry and I can hear it. She doesn't know you like that, but I do. You're not allowed to talk to her again if you're only going to call after you've been drinking," I say. Walking around to the driver's side of my car, I lean against the door. "She's completely innocent in everything between you and me, so don't play the victim with my daughter. She's not responsible for your emotions and neither am I. But you are. Figure your shit out and don't call her unless you're stone sober."

"She doesn't even know if she misses me, Elise. I'm her fucking dad," he yells.

"Yeah, you are, but how is she supposed to know if she misses you if she doesn't even know you?" I say. Looking through the window of my car, I see her facing away from me. Staring out her window with her favorite plush elephant smooshed against her chest, I suddenly can't breathe. "I have to go."

I hang up without saying another word. He's no longer worth my words.

Chapter 14

DAMIAN

"My girls are here!" I exclaim as soon as Avery busts through the main door of the house from the garage.

Without dropping her bag or elephant, Avery throws herself into my arms, but it's not her normal "I'm so happy I'm here with all your toys" kind of hug. This is a stage-five clinger kind of hug and I momentarily wonder if I read the situation wrong.

"What happened?" I demand as soon as Elise is in the house.

"Tanner called," she says. "We'll talk about it later. She didn't speak the entire drive here."

I hold Avery tighter, her head buried in the crease of my neck and shoulder, and nod in response to Elise's statement. Elise steps out of her sandals and puts them by the door and the next thing I know, she's joined our hug. I hold them both as best I can, shifting Avery to my hip so I can wrap my free arm around Elise.

"You know what we need?" I ask.

Avery sniffles against my shoulder.

"Ice cream?"

And Elise and I laugh, because ice cream seems to fix everything for these ladies.

"We can do ice cream later. I was actually thinking dinner on the deck, though," I say. "You want to help me make the grilled cheese while Mom gets out plates? How about some chocolate milk?"

She nods against my shoulder and squeezes me as hard as her little arms can before letting go.

"You give the best hugs, Damian."

"Well, thank you, Aves. I try to practice as much as possible," I say, placing a kiss on her temple and setting her feet on the floor.

Elise has already pulled plates from the cupboard and busied herself with hulling strawberries. While the pan heats for grilled cheese, I grab down a glass for Avery's drink and pull the chocolate sauce from the fridge.

"Two or three flavors tonight, ladies?" I ask. "I stopped at the cheese store, so we can go wild if you want. I refuse to settle for just plain old American ever if I can help it."

I watch as they exchange a look, then a smile, before they reply in unison.

"Go wild."

It isn't life altering — to most people — but I've lived my whole life wishing for moments like this. Elise is the only one who's ever given them to me. She spends time with me and includes me in her world. I could be making a million dollars a year, and none of it would matter if I could guarantee my work day ending with family time. Maybe I'll get my wish after all.

*****

Dinner was amazing. We made six different kinds of grilled cheese and then shared all of it. There's some leftover for Avery to have at home along with the extra strawberries, but she was in her glory between helping make dinner and then getting to try all the combinations she created.

It wasn't until Aves was full and asked to be excused from the table that Elise finally opened up about the phone call with Tanner. His drunk phone call. He's more of an asshole when he's been drinking and I've known that since the first time I met him. Unfortunately, it took Elise a little longer to figure it out.

"I never liked him. He didn't treat you well. He's always been toxic. And if I'm being honest—"

"As if you haven't always been honest," she interrupts, laughing and grabbing the plate out of my hand as I finish washing it so she can rinse and set it in the drainboard.

I stop what I'm doing to assess the situation and figure, fuck it, I've already opened my stupid mouth.

"Not this honest, Elise. He's a shitty dad. The only reason I've stuck around even though my sister had made plans and was moving away and my parents live far enough away that if I up and moved it wouldn't be a shock to them ... the only reason I stayed was to make sure Avery had a decent male role model other than your dad," I say, my voice barely rising, but the tone is telling of my frustration. "You both deserve so much more.

You deserve a man who's going to love you for you and take care of you and your daughter to the best of his ability. Tanner was never going to be that guy. Ever. He can't even take care of himself."

When I'm done with my tirade my heart is pounding and I'm a little out of breath. I try not to get too emotional, but lately it's difficult to hold it in. The shock on her face doesn't make me feel confident about my declaration, but she needed to know how I felt. Especially if I'm going to be a bigger part of her life and Avery's. I've always been part of their lives, but it's more now. This baby is going to connect us forever, and we've hardly begun the journey.

Her silence makes it hard for me to be quiet, too. If she's not going to respond, then I'm just going to keep going.

"There was nothing else tying me here for all these years. Nothing. Most of my clients live in my computer, Elise, or are at least far enough away that I should have relocated at some point. Could have. I could have relocated somewhere that isn't cold eight months of the year. I could be sitting on a beach designing houses and buildings for these people and fly wherever they need me. But I couldn't because I would have missed seeing Avery. I would have missed you."

"Why are you telling me this?"

Does she really have no idea even after all the time we've spent together, after our trip to New York City, after planning and creating and implanting a tiny life inside her … after last night?

Scrubbing my hands down my face, I feel the three days growth of stubble and it doesn't even faze me that I should shave. It isn't a big deal because she's said she likes me scruffy. Frustrated, I push my hands up into my hair and consider all the things I wanted to talk to her about tonight. All the things I claimed were "neutral" and not a huge deal.

It's absolutely a huge deal. It's always been a huge deal and that's why I haven't ever brought it up.

"What is it about this conversation, about talking about her father, that makes this part of you come out of hiding?" she asks.

She's killing me here. Her voice is so small and I never want to make her feel like she needs to shrink herself to fit in my space.

"Because you're carrying my baby and you're my reason to stay. You. I haven't run away from home since the day I met you," I say, stepping into her bubble. Placing my hands on either side of her neck and looking in her eyes, I say, "I didn't need to run away. But he got all the parts of you I wish I had the courage to ask for years ago. I've been in love with you since I was nineteen, Elise."

A slight gasp escapes, but her features soften. She opens her mouth to say something and immediately closes it.

"What?" I ask, hearing the fear in my voice.

My body is on alert, afraid she's going to tell me I'm crazy and I'm not supposed to love her as more than a friend. What if she doesn't feel the same way? What if this is all too much? What if she panics and calls my sister? Fooling around because her hormones have her seeking a release is one thing. Telling her I love her? That escalates things.

"You've been holding that in for a decade?" she asks.

"Just about. I mean, it's more like thirteen years, but who's counting."

I gently brush my thumbs along her jaw, trying to memorize every detail of her in case this is the last time I get to touch her in such an intimate way. In case I just fully screwed up our entire friendship, I need to make a memory.

Releasing a sigh, Elise grips my beltloops. I take that as an invitation to stop worrying about the lines I'm constantly crossing, because I've gotten really good at crossing them. Dropping my forehead to hers, I get the feeling things will be okay. For now.

"Thirteen years? Not once did you say anything like that. You never gave any clear indication there was more than just best friend kind of caring about me. You kept your distance, a lot at times, and I'm sure there were reasons, but it was so ... confusing," she whispers. "Why not say anything? It could have saved us so much time."

Pushing her chin up with my thumbs I look directly in her hazel eyes, noticing the flecks of green and gold for the hundredth time since I first saw her as more than just my little sister's best friend, and I consider my words carefully.

"It would have never worked back then. We both needed time to figure out who we are," I say. Her forehead wrinkles and I know she's considering all the ways she already knew who she was at sixteen. "I never would have jeopardized your future for my own gain. You had dreams and goals. I knew where I was headed, but I needed you to get where you wanted to be."

She swallows hard and I release her chin.

"Was this what you wanted to talk to me about tonight?"

I nod, because I'm too afraid if I start talking again, I won't stop in an effort to make sure she knows how I feel because me just telling her might not be enough.

"I see why you went with 'neutral.' This could have gone very, very badly if I didn't feel the same way about you."

"You feel the same way?"

She smirks. She raises her eyebrow. Then her tongue darts out and dampens her bottom lip.

"Since I was about … sixteen. But you were in college and then you were an adult. Then Angela and I were in college and being grownups. Even with you around, it was difficult to admit how I felt," she says.

I'm floored by the fact we've been skirting around our attraction and feelings for more than a decade without figuring it out or at least trying to bring it up to one another.

"Then, I was with Tanner and I tried to forget about you, even with you right there. I didn't want to admit I was settling for the band boy who had no plan for a future other than jamming with his buddies every weekend."

"But without him, we wouldn't have Avery, and she's pretty amazing. I wouldn't give her up to do it differently," I say.

"Neither would I. Just like I wouldn't give up what we're doing now for you, to make you a dad, to go back and do it differently. I don't think this would work without all the other pieces," she says, placing her hand on my cheek. "And after last night … I think we're both figuring out we're the final pieces."

"Like a LEGO house?" I ask, pulling her closer to me.

"Um … or a puzzle."

"Tab A into slot B?" I joke as she presses against my body, fitting into me like she was meant to all along.

"Dirty. But we're going to get there," she says, and I know the moment she feels me. "Probably not tonight. Avery has school in the morning and I need to go to work. A sleepover might not be the best idea."

I agree with her, but I'm still sad about it.

"So, before I let go of you and we try to have a normal, not filled with sexual tension, kind of evening, is this the official 'we're dating' conversation? Or …"

"I think it's safe to say this is as official as it gets."

95

That's all the permission I need to back her up against the kitchen counter, and let her mouth find mine. She wraps her arms around my neck as I lift her to sit beside the sink and her legs find their way around my waist. Pulling her bottom lip between my teeth, she places her hands on my face and takes control, deepening the kiss. It's the best feeling in the world to taste her and know she's mine.

Breathlessly, after pulling away from her mouth, I say, "I just want you to know, I'm not saying all of this because of what happened before you got here tonight or because you said you'd carry my baby. If you hadn't made the first move, I never would have told you, but last night kind of pushed me over the edge. In more ways than one."

I stare at her for a moment, feeling the energy radiate off her, then add, "And I didn't choose you to carry my baby because I love you. You know that, right?"

"I'm pretty sure I know that. Just like I didn't ask you to choose me because I love you. It's because I didn't want you to have to try to trust someone you didn't know. I know how difficult that is for you."

"Good. Okay. Good," I say, trying to get my bearings back.

"Are you sure? Maybe you should kiss me again, just to be extra certain you're good," she says.

Taking her lips tenderly against mine again, I know she's the only one I want to kiss like this for the rest of my life. Pulling away, I look her in the eyes and nod.

"Definitely good."

Chapter 15

ELISE

Life has carried on like normal — as normal as we can have it, anyway.

Damian and I are taking everything slow. Molasses slow. We're both okay with that, too. I think taking everything one day at a time is smart since we have a lot going on. We rushed into our relationship, but didn't really rush into it considering all the years we've known one another. Moving our friendship to the next level and sprinkling the romance in feels natural.

We've spent more time focusing on adjusting to the way my body is responding to this pregnancy than anything else. He's asked questions and, honestly, it feels nice to have someone care about how pregnancy is affecting me.

It's been six weeks since we opened up to one another about our feelings and right around that time, the morning sickness hit full force, my chest got more tender and painful to the point I need to wear a bra nonstop to keep it from hurting just by moving, and I began praying to any and every god to get me through the first trimester without losing both my jobs from the insane levels of exhaustion.

The one thing that's gotten me through is the ultrasound a few weeks after the positive test. Seeing the flicker of a heartbeat on the screen and watching Damian's face go from scared to awestruck was amazing. I know this baby isn't mine. There's zero chance of me being "mom." But to watch my boyfriend fall in love with his little bean maybe makes me hopeful for us to have one together at some point.

I never experienced any of this with Tanner. He wasn't even at my first ultrasound with Avery. No one held my hand.

But Damian has.

They are night and day.

I am well aware of how unrealistic our entire situation is. How often does this actually happen where a surrogate starts dating the intended parent?

"What are you thinking about?" he asks from the doorway.

Avery and I are at his house for dinner again, and instead of asking me to help in the kitchen he insisted I go rest in the living room while Avery oscillates between playing and helping him here and there with little things.

"Things I shouldn't be thinking about," I say, biting the inside of my cheek before adding, "If I'm honest, they're things I should have thought about a while ago."

Pulling the towel off his shoulder and wiping his hands, he leans against the doorframe. His broad shoulders taking up more space than I thought possible. He was such a nerdy guy when we were younger. Now ... he's still nerdy, but also muscular and athletic. He's nothing like the guys I used to date, in intelligence or physique. Him being completely different from anyone else in my past is exactly what kept me from realizing his feelings for me.

"Do you want to talk about it?" he asks, glancing behind him at Avery, who's in the kitchen setting the table.

"Only if you want to."

He surrenders and comes to the couch. It's deep enough to fit both of us if we lay on our sides. I scoot back into the cushions to make room for him.

"You smell like apples," I say.

"That's a good thing then, since I made applesauce to go with dinner."

"You made applesauce? Like, cut up apples and made sauce? From scratch?" I ask, unable to hide my amusement. Mostly it's because I only half believe he would do something like that.

"Yes. I went to the farmer's market and bought fresh apples and brought them home, peeled and chopped them, and then cooked them. Applesauce."

Reaching up to touch his face, I feel so exhausted. Trailing my finger down his cheek, I wonder out loud, "How did I get this lucky?"

He smiles, turning his face into my palm and planting a kiss to the center.

"I ask myself the same thing every time I hold your hair while you throw up," he says, his tone silly but the words full of meaning. "So, what's on your mind?"

I sigh, because this wasn't a conversation I thought we would have. Not today, and not really ever.

"Do you think we're being overzealous?"

"About what?"

"Being in a relationship when I'm your surrogate and you're—" ugh, how do I say the next part gently? I can't. I can't say it other than to just say it. "When you're paying me. Is this weird? You're paying me to carry your baby, but then we're also dating, and I don't want anyone to get stupid ideas like you're paying me to be your girlfriend."

I notice his eyebrows knit together and wish I had stopped talking before I even started. But does that stop me from continuing? Of course not.

"How often do surrogates find themselves in a situation like this? Where they end up with the parent they're incubating a baby for? I worry you're going to get in trouble. Does your attorney know about this? Mine doesn't and she'd probably have a fucking coronary."

His right eyebrow raises slightly while waiting for me to finish. When I do stop talking it's because I'm crying.

"I hate this part. I just want to cry about everything. A kid dropped an entire tray of paint cups today and I had to leave the room after cleaning it up because I was inconsolable. Yesterday, I cried because my favorite socks weren't clean," I say, sucking in a breath in a futile attempt to control the sobbing. It doesn't work and I hiccup through saying, "They weren't clean because I'm a grown up and have to do my own laundry!"

If anything, this should prove to him I'm not relationship material. Right? Instead, he gathers me up in his arms the best he can while we're still laying on the couch, and rocks until he's on his back and I'm laying half on top of him and half on the couch.

"Do you need me to go across town and get your dirty clothes and wash them?" he asks quietly as he brushes my hair from my cheek. I grasp his dress shirt in my hand and then smooth it out only to rub my index finger along the seam of the shirt opening, pressing it gently until it's flattened against his chest.

"No," I sniffle. "I'm an adult. I can do it."

"So, which part is bothering you most? Missing favorite socks, dating me, or the idea of people thinking I'm paying you to carry a baby and date me?"

His words are quiet and I hear everything he isn't saying. The fear that I'm going to say it's him.

"It's not you," I respond automatically. "Maybe it really isn't any of it. I'm just so afraid something bad is going to happen now that we're together."

"Like?"

"Like I'll deliver this little person and you'll decide you don't really want to play house after all."

He's quiet. Fresh tears slip down my face to be quickly absorbed by his shirt. Time slows down.

"When is your lease up?" he asks out of left field.

Lifting my head from his chest, I find his deep brown eyes staring at me.

"Why?" I whisper, though I already have a good idea.

"Just ... when is it up?"

"November. The fifteenth."

"Okay."

"Why?" I ask again.

He wraps his arms around me securely, kisses my forehead, and shrugs.

"You're not the only one with a lot on your mind. That's all."

I laugh, wiping the last of my tears away.

"I don't know if I'm ready to give up the freedom of having my own place, Damian. If that's what you're insinuating," I say. "That would be a big change for Avery, too. Her school district won't change, which is good since she just started Pre-K and I don't want to take her from the new friends she's making, but ..."

"I get it. But that's why I asked when the lease renews. This would give you and Aves two months to get used to the idea, and you could start slowly moving things over here," he says. "This isn't a knee-jerk request or a reaction to your concerns. I've put a lot of thought into it."

Of course, I know it's not a rash decision. Damian isn't the kind of guy to go into something like this lightly. Just like he spent months, maybe even years, considering surrogacy, I imagine he's spent every bit of the last six weeks wondering when would be the right time to ask about my lease.

We continue laying together quietly on the couch as Avery wanders back in. She pops over to us, throwing her little body on top of us in a ramshackle hug, before picking a baby doll up off the chair and heading in the direction of Damian's office. He twists his neck enough to watch her go before looking back at me.

"Plus, she already has a room here and has been getting acquainted with it," he says.

"She what?"

"That wasn't intentional. She was helping me in the baby's room when you were working at the diner a few weeks ago. I've been painting. She loves to paint. I wasn't going to tell her no," he says. I sit up as best I can, my legs straddling his thighs, and give him a scorching look as I wait for him to continue. "It's a four-bedroom house, Elise."

As if that makes it make sense? As if that makes it okay?

"She wants a place for her toys when the two of you are here and neither of us want to trip over them all day long. There's nothing wrong with me giving her her own space," he says, further explaining. "I should have done it sooner. Avery has been in my life as long as I've been in hers and long before we were together, she spent enough time here that I should have made a better playroom for her instead of just having that little nook."

"Am I allowed to be mad about it?" I say, crossing my arms over my chest.

"No. You aren't. And if you are, you can call Angela and talk to her about it," he says, placing his hands on my hips and sliding me up his legs. "She already knows and thought it was brilliant."

My best friend is a traitor.

"And you aren't afraid we're moving way too fast?"

He bites his lower lip then shakes his head.

"Nope."

"She knows you gave Avery her own room here, but did you tell her we're a thing?"

That's something we haven't taken the time to do. Alerting his sister to our budding relationship hasn't been a priority between working two jobs and being pregnant, Avery starting school, and Damian having a sudden uptick in design requests. We fell into this naturally, but Angela doesn't live here now and so misses out on the day-to-day stuff. Should we make an effort to tell her? Absolutely, because she's going to be crushed if she doesn't hear it from us.

"I did not tell her. I think we should do it together. She's coming home next weekend, so I figured what's a few more days. We can do dinner, I'll make her favorite foods and butter her up before I tell her I'm banging her bestie," he says, barely able to contain his laughter.

"You're ridiculous," I say, but his reaction is infectious and I find myself giggling along with him. "The only issue with saying it like that is you haven't even reached third base and it's all your baby's fault."

He gently touches the small swell of my abdomen, then pulls me even higher up his body until he can wrap his arms around my waist. Damian lifts his head and touches his forehead to my belly. My fingers find his hair, twisting the short strands between my fingers, as I feel his lips press against my shirt in the most tender kiss.

"Can you do me a favor, little dude? Maybe chill out just a little?" he whispers against me. "I know you're growing really fast right now, and it takes a lot for you to get strong, but we're really hoping you settle down in the next trimester. I know Elise would love to not fall asleep before dinner most nights."

He glances up at me, a smirk appearing as the corners of his eyes crinkle ever so slightly. I stay quiet, wondering if he's going to make a male plea for sex to finally happen. I've lived through that. It's not attractive and I don't do guilt sex, but I'm careful not to let my thoughts display on my face.

"Plus, if she's able to think clearly," he says, resuming the conversation with my belly, "maybe she'll see it's not silly for me to want her to live here with us. I'm crazy in love with her and that's why I want her in all my spaces. Not because I want her freedom. I love her for exactly who she is."

I attempt to swallow the lump in my throat. I'm unsuccessful and swallow again.

"Talking like that will ruin me for any other man, Damian," I say, the joke being lost by the coming onslaught of emotion.

"I don't intend on any other man having you, Elise."

Chapter 16

DAMIAN

On October fourth, my sister pulls in my driveway, storms into my house and immediately makes a beeline for the full bathroom that's tucked away between the kitchen and the living room.

She didn't even yell a hello through the house. The only reason I know it's her is because I got an alert on my phone from the security camera and can see her car. Looking closely at the image, I'm not even sure she turned it off, but am grateful she at least put it in "park" so she doesn't roll down the hill and into the lake.

"Daaaaaamiiiiiiiian!" she screams from the bathroom.

Lifting myself up out of my office chair, I save the files I'm working on, and make my way casually through the house from the workroom.

"Aaaaaaangelaaaaaaa!" I yell back, mocking her.

Wandering into the kitchen with my water bottle, I go to the sink and refill it. There's a candle lit on the kitchen table and my mouth automatically smiles because Elise must have lit it before she left after lunch. We've been trying to make Friday lunch at home our thing. It's helping her get more used to the idea of moving in. She's still a little on the fence, and I'm not pushing. If she chooses to renew her lease, that's her prerogative and I'll support her. But I want her to feel like this is home, too.

The bathroom door flies open and I hear my sister before I see her.

"Do you need to tell me something?" she asks.

When I look up, I see her holding a teal bathrobe and she knows it isn't mine. For starters, I don't wear bathrobes. Second, I'm more of a dark green person. Third, I have a feeling I'll be breaking the news to her without Elise here, which might be for the best.

"I'm unsure. Do you think I need to tell you something?" I lift an eyebrow at her and take a swig of my water.

"This isn't yours, so whose is it? Mom doesn't leave stuff here," she says. As another thought crosses her mind, she gasps and angrily asks, "Did you get a girlfriend while Elise is pregnant? Are you stupid?"

Squinting at her, I wait. I'm definitely the smarter of the two of us so …

I'll play her game though.

"And what if I did?" I ask.

Her face falls. She drops her arm, and the long end of the bathrobe pools on the floor.

"But ..."

I stare at her waiting for her to continue. I know she will. My sister doesn't ever stay quiet long.

"You have a baby on the way. Why would you keep trying to date? Does she know? It's got to be serious if she's leaving things here," she says, sounding a little less mad but definitely upset still. "And quick. You weren't even seeing anyone last time I was home and you do not move into relationships quickly. You never have."

"You want something to eat? I'm almost done with work and then have to get ready to go get Avery. You can ride with me if you want."

"I'm not hungry. And what about Avery? She's got her own room here and that can't look good to a new girlfriend. The daughter of your sister's best friend, who's also your surrogate, has her own room at your house," she says, slowly piecing things together but not quite getting it. So close. See? I told you I was the smarter one. "Is she a freaking saint?"

I make a thoughtful expression and then slowly nod.

"Yeah, she kind of is. Seriously, food. I made your favorite," I say, pulling a pan of salted caramel brownies from the oven. "I even added extra caramel pieces on top."

Reluctantly, she walks over to the table and hangs the bathrobe on the back of a chair.

"I feel like you're about to break some sort of news to me," she says, reaching for the pan in my hand.

Handing her a knife, I ask her to please not stab me.

"It would look really bad if you did. You know, to my girlfriend who's an amazing person and I think you're going to love," I say. I turn away from Angela so she can't see my smile and pour her a glass of milk. "Sit. We'll talk."

"I don't like when you want to talk. You're going to be all big brother to me and I don't know if I can handle that shit today. It was a long drive from Buffalo."

I scrunch my nose at her.

"I still don't know why you took a job in Buffalo. Aren't there colleges here you could have found a job at?"

"Yes, but I wanted to be able to spread my wings and all that. I worked at the community college and it was great, but I didn't see myself staying there long term. You know this. Plus, they didn't have anything in student affairs open and when this other job came up ... can we just leave it alone?" she asks, looking like she's on the verge of tears. "I already have Mom upset still that I moved."

She breaks apart a brownie and places a piece in her mouth, savoring it.

"Tell me about this girlfriend. Does she know about the baby?"

"She's local, works at a school, is amazing."

"That tells me absolutely nothing. Does Elise know? She works at a school ... Jesus, Damian, does Elise know her?"

"She does," I say, smiling. I feel the heat rise in my cheeks.

"And Avery? You can't date someone seriously without Avery's approval. She's practically your shadow."

"Pretty sure she knows."

Angela sighs.

"Okay, just fucking out with it. If she's local I've got to know her. This town isn't that big, Damian."

"Oh, you definitely know her," I say. Waiting until her mouth is full, I add, "You could even say she's your closest friend outside of me, your amazing and wonderful older brother."

She stops chewing. Her eyes go wide. Then she looks at the bathrobe on the chair beside her, glances at the candle on the table, spies the extra pair of shoes Elise left at the house, and a picture of the three of us — me, Elise, and Avery — hanging on the fridge along with the sonogram picture.

"You and Elise? You're dating Elise? My best friend? The woman carrying my niece or nephew? That Elise?"

With my water bottle halfway to my mouth, I pause to gauge her reaction. Is it good? Bad? Unsure? I'm unsure, that's for sure.

"Don't murder me?" I ask of her.

I don't move, except to lower my arm and wait for her to say something more. Her eyes are pensive, giving off a vibe somewhere between things will be okay and "Mom's going to kill you, not me."

"Why her?"

The question throws me off, and I cock my head slightly to the side.

"Why not her?"

"I love Elise, she's been my best friend for more than half my life, Damian. But ... you couldn't have picked any other person to date? You had to pick my best friend? What happens when you fuck it up?"

"Whoa. Who says anyone is going to mess this up?" I ask, defensively.

"Someone always messes it up."

I take that as my cue to sit, and pull out the chair across from my sister. Settling myself, I fold my hands together so I don't fidget.

"She has never once given any indication she was into you," she says. "Well, not never, but I never thought she was serious about a crush on you."

Angela throws her head back and groans, as if she had missed all the signs and she's just now seeing them for what they were.

"Can I ask you something?"

"Sure. Why not? You've kind of got me as a captive audience, D."

"Before Tanner, how often did Elise go out with anyone? A date? A relationship?"

She narrows her eyes at me, popping another piece of brownie in her mouth.

"Pretty much never," she says. "Why?"

I can't deal with this and I hate mind games as much as the next guy, so I just come out with it.

"I've had feelings for her since we were teenagers. Apparently, she's felt the same way. Neither of us knew that and we focused more on our friendship, because that's important to both of us. When she met Tanner, she figured that was it," I say, watching as it clicks for her that this isn't a relationship of convenience. "Before you start worrying that Elise said yes to being my surrogate because of her feelings for me, no. Our feelings for one another were not the reason she offered or I accepted."

"But it seems pretty freaking coincidental that she'd offer knowing she had feelings that didn't align with a 'he's just a friend' mentality," she scoffs.

I'll give her that. But, I also didn't have to say yes and agree.

"Neither of us had to sign that contract, you know. I need you to get it. Understand, Angela. I've found no one else who fits me like she does. Years wasted on dates with all the wrong people. Please. Understand."

"I do," she says, relenting. "I can't be mad. I'm confused as hell, but I can't be mad. What happens when the baby is born?"

Taking a moment to collect my thoughts, because I have thought about this, I make her wait for the answer. And the answer is simple.

"We keep living life because, baby or no baby, Elise and Avery are a huge part of mine."

*****

It's close to dinner before I hear from Elise. When she calls, it's to ask what time I'm going to swing by the diner and grab Avery for the night. After finding out Avery has her own room at the house, we had a small family meeting. That conversation turned into a shopping trip for a new bed and dresser.

Elise warned me that once I started buying things for Avery I wouldn't stop, but I've been buying things for her since the minute she was born and I've never had any reason to not continue. Whatever logic she was attempting isn't working. The rocking chair in her bedroom at the apartment? I bought that. I also went out and bought a car seat like I said I would because swapping Elise's in and out of vehicles was a pain in the ass.

"Is it okay if Angela comes with me?" I ask, having wandered away from my sister and into my office so she can't hear me on the phone. "She's been home a few hours. Stopped here first instead of going to Mom and Dad's."

"Oh. ... Oh no."

"Oh yes."

"How did she take it? She hasn't texted or called to scream at me. That isn't good," she says, keeping her voice as even as possible, but failing miserably at it. "That's not good. She's mad, isn't she?"

I would make her sweat it out a minute, but I can hear the emotion in her voice. Freaking out. Not okay. She's going to be in tears if I make her wait.

"No," I say as succinctly as possible. "She's not mad at you. Or me. She's stressed out about work and we're confusing and she's worried that after the baby is born everything will be weird now that we're together since you're not biologically related to him. Or her. Them."

This not knowing what we're having is more difficult than I expected. I don't want to know sex until birth, though, so I swap constantly and make people question things.

"If you ask me, I think she's just angry she didn't put it all together sooner or on her own," I add for good measure.

"Okay, as long as she's not angry and going to cause a scene or anything bring her with you. Otherwise, I won't get to see her until tomorrow."

Awesome. It's settled. We'll meet them at the diner, probably grab milkshakes, and then come home. Avery can eat, then get ready for bed and have a movie night with Aunt Angela while I finish up some work. Elise should be home around midnight, she'll shower, and get some sleep.

"We're doing brunch tomorrow?" I ask.

"Only if you let me sleep in."

"Brunch it is. I'll see you in a bit. I love you," I say, then wait for her response and hang up. Switching gears, I walk back to the kitchen and say to my sister, "Wanna ride with me to get Aves? Elise said yes to brunch in the morning, so I figured if there's something specific you want, we can stop and pick it up."

"Perfect," she says, her eyes not leaving her open laptop screen.

"Did you bring work home with you?"

"No. Yes ... it's not work work. It's for a class I'm auditing."

My mouth forms an O because I'm not sure how to respond. My sister is intelligent, but not studious.

"It's a psychology course."

"Interesting," I say, lifting one shoulder and turning to walk away again.

"Damian?" she asks, encouraging me to turn back to face her. "Did you tell her I kind of freaked out?"

Shaking my head, I know my expression makes it look like I'm questioning her. She really didn't freak out any more than I thought she would and, if I'm being honest, I was expecting way worse. Angela argues dirty and I wouldn't have been surprised if she'd called me names. I'm glad she didn't, but I just know it's not beneath her.

"I didn't mean to make you feel like you didn't know what you were doing or that you were doing something wrong. I just ... I know what she's been through with Tanner. All the sordid details. So, I'm a little protective of her and Avery. I know you aren't anything like him and I shouldn't just assume it won't work for you two," she says, closing her computer and standing so we're face-to-face. "I love both of you and am happy you've both found someone who makes you happy."

Opening my arms, my baby sister finds her way over to me and I wrap her up in my embrace.

"If you hurt her," she says, her voice muffled against my shirt, "I will murder you and no one will find your body."

"For starters, you didn't make me feel like that," I say. Kissing her on the temple, I add, "For seconds, duly noted, but I have no intentions of ever hurting her. Thirds, you'll find your penguin soon enough."

Her laughter shakes us both. "My penguin?"

"They mate for life … and if you're lucky enough to find an Emperor penguin, they're in charge of the egg until it hatches."

"Avery has you watching Wild Kratts again?"

"She does, but that's beside the point," I say, pushing her away. "Chocolate milkshakes are on me. Get your shoes and we'll go to the diner."

Chapter 17

ELISE

"Why would you threaten him?"

"Because he's my big brother and I'm allowed to," Angela says, slowly slipping her straw in her mouth and attempting to look innocent.

I'm not on break, but it's slow for the moment so I stopped to visit with Ang while she sips her milkshake. Her natural state of standing behind the counter with me just happened even though she no longer works here, and Mac does a doubletake when he walks out from the kitchen.

"Kid! What are you doing home, Angela? I thought you left us for one of those bigger cities?"

Her face lights up as he grabs her and pulls her in for a hug. Mac is the extra uncle/dad figure we all needed growing up.

"I did, but with a new baby coming, I needed to come home so I don't miss out on all of the excitement," she says, then sticks her tongue out at me.

"Yeah, she told me. Think she'll work right up until she goes into labor again like with Avery?"

I feel my face heat. Mac told me for a week straight to take some time off, but I couldn't afford to miss out on the tips. I had spent my entire pregnancy saving them so I could afford to be off work with a newborn and not get behind on rent. He finally yanked my tables from me and sent me to the hospital when he noticed I was cringing and not talking through contractions.

"I'm going to try to not do that again, okay. It wasn't fun the first time," I say, interjecting before they can get carried away. "Plus, this time I'm not taking care of a freeloader ex-boyfriend along with myself."

Mac winks at me, then says, "Nah, this time you're the freeloader."

His bellowing laugh is the only reason I don't offer to let him take my shift for the night while I go put my feet up. He's such a good guy and I know he's teasing, but it's no secret I'm worried people will think I'm taking advantage of Damian. I've given Mac a majority of the details about the agreement and contract, right down to the dollar amount. He's always worried I won't have the money to keep Avery fed and clothed well, so that information put him at ease.

"That's horrible Mac. Be kind," Angela says through her laughter.

"I'm just kidding. I have nothing but love for you and Avery," he says to me. "The three of you. You're my girls. Life wouldn't be the same without you and your shenanigans."

"Same," Damian says, climbing onto a barstool at the counter. He looks me square in the face and, as seriously as he can manage, says, "Avery is busy. She's coloring a new picture for Mac's office and will join us when she's done. That's a direct quote."

"Sassy little monster," Angela says, snickering. "Okay, so while we wait for her, what can I do to help around here?"

Mac and I look at her like she's got three heads.

"Nothing. You're a guest. Not on the payroll right now. Sit and enjoy your shake," Mac says, then offers her one more of his famous hugs before wandering into the kitchen, leaving the three of us standing around awkwardly.

"It feels weird to have you here but not be working with you, you know that right?" I say to Angela.

"Oh, I absolutely know. It's weird for me, too. I'm itching to clean a table or reorganize the sugar packets. It's killing me," she says. "I don't have a lot of little busywork kind of things like that at my job now. And there's some clique-y shit with some of the people in the building I work in."

"Is that the reason for the class you're auditing?" Damian asks.

I look from one to the other. Angela didn't tell me she was thinking about taking any classes, so it comes as a bit of a shock. She didn't love college the first time, so it's surprising she'd take a class on purpose for no credit.

"Yup. I'm trying to figure out how their brains work because they just don't work like normal. Or maybe I'm just lucky and didn't have to put up with shit like that when we were younger. I don't know. Maybe the class will lead to something bigger for me."

"I'm going to go with we were fortunate and didn't deal with the whole mean girl thing very often," I say. "It's the same thing at my school, though. Except for Julia and Laura. They don't seem to be part of those circles."

A quirked eyebrow from Angela but no verbalized question has me questioning her. The typical, "What?" when something suddenly feels off; when the vibe shifts.

"Who's Julia?"

Ah ... I rarely talk about the other people at work, so she only knows Laura. They've met a few times over the years I've worked at the school, like on days Avery ended up sick and I needed someone to come pick her up. Aunt Ang to the rescue.

"She started around the time you moved," I explain. "I don't know her too well, but she's definitely trying to find her people at work. Friend seeking and whatnot, but she's getting in with the rowdy teacher crowd. If I can save her from that, I'll do my best."

I say crowd as if there are a hundred of us employed there. There aren't. We just have been blessed with a small handful of teachers who think talking shit about their co-workers is the flex of the century.

"You're not replacing me, are you?" Angela asks.

I let out a laugh, then realize how serious she is. She drops her gaze to stare into her milkshake cup.

"No. No one can replace you. What's this about?" I ask, looking at Damian who shrugs at me. Angela is good at not letting on when something bothers her, so this behavior is out of place, especially at the diner. "No one is replacing anyone. You're my best friend and part of my family. What's actually going on?"

She sets her cup on the counter and raises her arms, then laces her fingers and places them on top of her head. She shrugs, just like her brother did.

"That's not going to work," I say.

"I don't know. I don't know what's wrong," she responds, unconvincingly.

"Liar, liar, pants on fire," Damian blurts out in a sing-song voice.

It's not that I don't agree with him, but as I stand here watching the tears well up in her eyes while she tries to maintain her composure ... something is definitely wrong.

Taking a deep breath, she says quickly, "I hate it there. I miss home. I don't know why I moved away. I don't like adventures on my own and it was stupid to think I could do this without you with me."

"So, your mood isn't because you haven't found the penguin yet?" Damian asks.

Twisting my head to look at him, I catch him in a death glare a split second before what he said registers. Then I scrunch my eyes and mouth, "What the fuck at you talking about?" He shrugs.

"No, stupid. It's got nothing to do with finding my one true love. You're such a weirdo," Angela says. "I think I made a mistake moving so far away."

We stand in the noise of the diner, looking at one another.

"Aunt Angela, I made you a picture for your 'rigerator," Avery says from beside Damian.

Climbing onto the barstool, Avery proceeds to tell Angela all about the picture. How it's the two of them at the lake, playing in the water, and swimming with fishes.

"And there's D's house, and Mommy and Damian are on the deck with the baby watchin' us," she says with finality.

Angela stares at the picture, which in reality is a few circles with arms and a large square topped with a triangle. But to Avery and Angela, it's a masterpiece and I know it's going to go directly onto the fridge when Ang gets back to Buffalo.

"Thank you, Sunshine. This is perfect," Angela says, leaning across the counter to kiss Aves on the forehead. "I love it."

"I'mma go draw more," Avery says, getting down from the counter.

Once she's out of earshot, Angela looks at me and says, "That's it. I'm moving back. I can't handle this. I'll come back and work here until I find a job in my field that's closer to home."

"I won't hire you back," I hear from the door behind me. "Don't pull that shit, Angela. You're a big girl and you can do this. It's just distance. It's a few hours in the car. Not like you can't stop along the way and explore the little towns. It doesn't have to be all Thruway driving."

"You ... won't hire me back?"

"Nope. You're better than working the counter at a diner. Only reason I keep your friend around is because I like her kid," Mac says, winking at me.

We all know what he's doing, because we all know if she isn't needed Angela won't press the issue. She's a fixer. She likes to come in and make things all better. There's nothing to improve at the diner.

"You're serious?"

"Fuck yeah, I am," Mac says. "Listen, we all believe in you. You need to believe in you, too. It's just a job out there. And, if the job isn't making you happy, find another one. Just not here."

"There are plenty of colleges between home and Buffalo. Pick a midpoint and check out what's in the area," I offer. "Even if you don't find something right away, you still have a job out there and you still have home right here. Give me and Damian somewhere to visit. Weekends away are nice, you know?"

Angela bites her lip, chewing on it a little as she thinks.

"I can do that," she says.

"Good, because I have tables to check on. Ang, nothing has changed much. We're still solving all our problems together. We'll get this figured out for you," I say, leaning in to kiss her cheek and give her a quick hug. Then a thought hits me. "Oh! Brockport is kind of in the middle. I mean it's more Buffalo way than here, but it's closer to home by at least an hour."

Her face lights up.

"I'll start a list," she says.

"Fabulous," I respond, and lift my hand up for a high five before turning to check my tables.

*****

Quietly opening the door, I slip my shoes off in the garage and sneak into the kitchen. I smell like fried food and old lady perfume. I'm thankful all the scents haven't made me throw up lately. Getting through the first trimester this time was hard — everything made me want to be sick, and running out of a classroom filled with curious three-year-olds so I could collect myself was interesting to say the least. At the diner, I can disappear if I need to catch my breath for a minute.

At school though, I try really hard not to let it show when smells are too strong. My kids are extremely observant and, at first, it was because I didn't want anyone to know my business. That's why only Laura knew what was going on when Damian and I first signed the contract. Now that I have a little bump started and the other teachers have picked up on all the signs ... let's just say the number of rumors I've heard about myself and who they think is the baby's father is an entirely different level of fuckery. I tend to keep my personal life under wraps when I'm at my day job. Considering they all know Avery's dad and I are not together, I've heard I've been knocked up by married dads of students, single dads of students, the delivery guy who is in the building at least twice a week, and that it was a one-night stand.

If only they really knew about all the planning and science that went into this little life. But that's not something they're privy to and I'm okay with that.

My mind wanders to all the things I wish I could say to the gossipy girls. I could say them ... I just don't want to give that kind of energy to them. Standing in the kitchen, as if it's my own space already, I pull my uniform shirt off over my head, folding and setting it on the counter. I unbutton the pants that are consistently getting more snug around my waist as my body adjusts to a new life growing inside. It's just another reminder to buy more maternity clothes. Then, grabbing the edge of the counter, I push my body away and stretch to release the tension in my back from standing all night.

The energy in the room shifts as I hear him pad into the kitchen on bare feet. I don't let on that I know he's here with me. I simply relish in his touch when he steps up behind me and trails his fingers up my backbone. I press back into him when his thumbs push into the tight muscles at the base of my spine and his fingers grasp my hips.

"What are you thinking about?" he asks, his voice hoarse with sleep.

"You and me," I whisper.

"What about you and me?" he asks, slowly pulling my hips back against him.

"I don't remember now," I say, pushing off from the counter and leaning into him as a more carnal desire sweeps through me.

Damian gently slides his left hand around to my abdomen and rests his palm on the swell of my exposed belly. The warmth of his skin, his breath on my neck, make my flesh pebble in anticipation. His lips connect with my collarbone as he slips his right hand around me and pulls me more snuggly against him. I hug him back, my left and right hands covering his, as we stand together.

"You really don't remember?" he asks, his lips tickling behind my ear.

"It really wasn't anything to do with us, just about us. People's perceptions. That's all."

"That sounds kind of heavy," he says, placing another kiss on the side of my neck. "Want to talk about it?"

My breath hitches and I wonder if he really wants to talk about it. Do I want to talk about it? Do I want to talk about it right now? When he could be taking me to bed and having a first with me? How have we been doing this — a relationship, a family, practically living together — for two months and not taken this step? We've done everything but. And I want to take this step. I want to get past the foreplay and then falling asleep before the best play.

"That's the last thing I want to do right now," I say. Pulling his right hand up to caress my breast, I feel him thicken against my backside. Everything has been so sensitive, he rarely gets to touch anything, but tonight all I want is for him to touch me everywhere. Turning my head to look at him, I say, "Can we please go to bed?"

His response is immediate as he gently pinches my nipple through the thin bra I have on and presses into me more as he walks me out of the kitchen. We barely make it into the bedroom before he pushes my zipper down. In one swift motion he turns me around and lays me on the bed, grabbing the waistband of my pants and underwear together and pulling them off my legs. He takes my sock off one foot and places my ankle on his shoulder, then takes the other one off, tossing them in the pile with my pants as he kisses his way from my ankle up to my calf and beyond.

I lightly laugh and then apologize for making him wait as long as we have.

"No apologizing," he says. "I would have waited forever for you to be ready if that's what you needed from me."

A gentle nip to the skin on my inner thigh as he slowly trails his fingers up the other leg. Then he switches and begins again as the rebellious need for me to take control begins to build. I don't let it win. I want him to worship every part of me and I release a sigh as his lips brush lightly against the sensitive area at the apex of my thighs. Watching his tongue dart out to touch, so carefully, and as he begins his descent to my core his gaze locks onto mine. I can't look away. I don't break eye contact with him until the sensation is so overwhelming that I can't keep my head from dropping back against the down comforter. Gripping the fabric while he slowly slips two fingers deep within me, my breath comes out in quick bursts, matching the rhythm he sets.

I want nothing between us. The fabric covering my breasts is all that remains on me and, sliding my arm behind me I quickly unhook the band. Baring everything to him, I pinch a nipple between each forefinger and thumb, twisting carefully as the feeling courses down my body bringing me closer to release.

So close.

But I don't want it to be over. We've waited so long for this.

Reaching down between my legs I find Damian's hair, my fingers twisting the locks until he releases my pussy and pushes himself up my body. His lips clamp down over one breast, his teeth grazing the tight nub prompts a low guttural moan from me. And then another as he presses his pelvis against me, trailing the fabric covering his erection against my vulva. Sliding my fingertips along his spine, I feel the top of his boxers and push them down his hips. Lifting his body higher above me, balancing on his hands, he drops a kiss to my lips as I unsheathe his cock and force the fabric down his thighs with my feet so he can kick them off to the pile of clothing beside the bed.

Breaking our connection, Damian settles his forehead against mine.

"I don't know if I'm going to last long, but I'm not focused on me," he says, closing his eyes. "I just want to make you feel good."

"You already have," I say, placing my palm against his cheek.

Angling his mouth over mine again, Damian's tongue opens my lips. I taste myself on him as the head of his cock grazes my entrance. His hips press forward and with each slow thrust, my orgasm builds. Each time he pulls back, I tighten around him, until we find a perfect pace and the only thing that matters is we're chasing each other over the precipice into bliss.

Damian wraps his arms under me, holding on as if he might lose me, and pumps his hips harder and faster as we reach the edge of our orgasms. As the first wave hits me, I bite down on his shoulder to keep from crying out and all at once his body stills.

"Fuck," he groans. "Oh fuck."

The muscles in my pussy contract, tightening around him, and I feel his cock pulse as he finds his release.

My body shudders against his as he slowly pulls out of me and quickly walks to the ensuite bathroom. Exhausted, I lay still, attempting to keep my eyes open and my mind awake enough to get myself to bed, when Damian comes back with a warm, damp washcloth. He carefully wipes down my thighs and is gentle with the tender flesh between my legs. I watch as he takes care of me, wishing I'd always had him. As he pulls the cloth away from my body, he catches me staring at him.

"What?" he asks, hoarsely.

"I've never had someone take care of me like you do."

"Elise ..." he says, but it's the emotion I hear more than my name. It's the way he says it. It's the love that comes with it. It's ... "I'll always take care of you."

He walks to the dresser and pulls out a clean pair of boxers for himself, slipping them on. Then he grabs another pair, along with one of his T-shirts, and dresses me in them.

"Promise?" I ask.

"Promise."

M.L. PENNOCK

Chapter 18

DAMIAN

We've reached the 26-week mark and ... I'm starting to freak out a little. Not because of any one thing in particular. I don't think so, anyway. It's probably because we're past the halfway mark and everything is starting to feel more real.

Elise and Avery officially moved in the rest of the way in the first weekend in November, we promptly put up Christmas decorations and then we spent Thanksgiving at our house with all of the family from both sides invited. It was a little much, I'll admit, but Angela was home, both our moms helped, and it was the first big memory we'll have together as an actual family.

Christmas came. Christmas went. Avery was beside herself with what we bought her and what Santa graciously provided, and she was equally excited to find little gifts for the baby. A pack of diapers under the tree, onesies that said "Little Brother" and "Little Sister" because we don't know who's growing in Elise's belly yet, and a few other small items. Nothing huge. I didn't buy the car seats or any of the big stuff I've put on the registry.

Yet.

We're in such a strange situation because technically, a baby shower would be for ... me? Every time I attempt to bring it up, it ends with Elise shutting down on me. She has been having a difficult time figuring out how we're managing that aspect of a traditional pregnancy. Usually, or it seems so anyway, there's a baby shower at some point and the problem we're running into really is deciding who the shower would be for. Or if we should have one at all. I figured if it was going to cause too much distress, we'd just skip it.

But, Angela.

Angela is on a different plane of existence than me right now. Angela is planning on throwing us a shower. Both of us, because, in my sister's words, "Duh."

And on New Year's Day, she announced as much. So here we are now, two weeks past that, and she's up our asses about themes and color schemes as she puts together invitations for everyone from our high school math teacher to my mom's best friend's sister-in-law. I wish I was joking.

"She's lost her damn mind," Elise says, looking over the list of names Ang sent her last night. "There are easily a hundred-fifty people on this list, Damian. This is nothing like when she helped plan the shower we had for Avery."

The frustration in her voice doesn't come as a surprise, but the sudden sobbing does. I turn from the sink, leaving the soapy dishes to be rinsed later, and walk over to the table. Wiping my hands down the front of my jeans, I look over Elise's shoulder at the list.

"I see, easily, fifteen names we can cross off."

"Really? Like who?" she counters.

I pick up the pen beside the printout of the email from Angela and begin slicing names off. One after another with no explanation why. It doesn't matter.

"Really? You don't want your best friend from college invited?" she asks, looking up at me through tear-coated eyelashes.

"Nope."

"Why?"

"Um ... because he hasn't spoken to me in like three years and has no idea I'm — we're — having a baby," I say. "Why would I have her invite someone I'm not even close to anymore? That's dumb. Just like I wouldn't invite him to my wedding because, again, we're not close anymore."

She stares at me, then sniffs before glancing back down at the paper.

Quietly, she asks, "Are you planning on getting married someday?"

Placing my hands on the table, on either side of her, I lean down until my lips press against her shoulder. Kissing her gently through the soft fabric of her shirt before turning my face to kiss her neck in the hollow below her ear, I whisper, "Someday."

"But today," I say leaning back to give her space, "we're worrying about why my insane sister wants to give us both headaches about a guest list."

Filled suddenly with a need I've never felt before that leaves me a little off kilter, I step away from Elise. Leaving her at the table with the list, I go back to the mundane task of washing dishes.

"I honestly think you could cross off half those names and none of them would be hurt about not getting an invite. We should just keep it to family and the closest friends," I say, my back to her.

"You said, 'I'm'," she says, quietly. So softly I would have missed it had I not turned the water off when I did.

"What?" I ask.

A sigh comes from deep within her, as if she's mustering the courage to repeat herself. We've been having a lot of moments like that lately. Little speed bumps of insecurity … like the night she cried herself to sleep in my arms after apologizing for being so big. She's having a baby. I, in no way, expected her to not look pregnant. It makes me worry about how Tanner really was with her when they were together. The reality is, I know very little about their relationship other than what I saw with my own eyes.

"You said you haven't spoken to your friend in years and he has no idea *you* are having a baby," she says.

As quickly as I can, I replay what I've said in the last five minutes.

"No, I said we're having a baby," I correct.

"No, Damian," she says, standing from the table and walking toward me. "You said you were having a baby and then you realized you slipped and fixed it, but you're right. You are having a baby. It's not my baby. You need to invite who you want to invite. This doesn't include me."

"Of course it includes you," I say, my voice rising slightly. "There would be no baby without you, Elise."

"I get that, but I'm just carrying him. Or her. That's my role. I'm not mom. I'm not anyone but Elise to this child," she says. "I'm just … I'm its dad's girlfriend."

We stare at one another and I try to put myself in her position.

"If we weren't in a relationship, if we weren't more than just friends, then yes. You'd just be Elise, the selfless girl who is giving me a family of my own. But you're so much more than that," I say, gripping the kitchen towel in my hands. "You might not be genetically its mom, but you're still in that role. Aren't you? You're not going to give birth to this kid and then move out and leave us, are you?"

Again, I hear my voice rising as the fear of losing her starts to seep in. Because that's a real fear I have now that I have her, that she's going to decide this isn't what she wants. That she doesn't want me after all. I clear my throat hoping it will call her attention up to my face.

She looks at her bare feet instead.

"Are you going to leave me?" I ask so softly I don't even sound like me to myself.

"No," she says. Sniffing, she raises her eyes to meet mine, "No, I'm not going to leave you. But I don't know what my place is, either. I'm struggling to figure out how I'll fit in this baby's life. We haven't talked about it, Damian. We haven't really broken down who I am. We've put ourselves in such a unique position that I don't know which end is up."

Swinging the towel over my shoulder to free up my hands, I step to her. My socked feet touching her bare toes with the chipped nail polish. Clasping her neck with both hands, I press and lift her chin with my thumbs so she has no choice but to look at me.

"Your place is with us. You're my family. You're this baby's family. And, if labels are that important to you? Then I want you to be Mom. Or Mommy. Or Mama. Pick one. Pick them all. You've nurtured this little person from the moment it was put in your body and you've loved it with everything you have either because you feel a connection to it or because that's just who you are — you are love — and I want you in their life for the rest of it. For all of it."

"But if something happens? I don't have legal rights to—"

"Stop right there. Woman, I am telling you right now, I'll give you all the rights you want. I'm willing to give you anything. I've always been ready to drop everything for you. Want take out for dinner? Great, me too. Want a new sweater? Let's go find one. Avery needs school supplies? Take me to Staples. Want my last name? It's yours. Let's go get married. Want to grow old and raise all the babies together regardless of DNA? I'm game."

Her eyebrows furrow and she cocks her head to one side.

"Are you hearing yourself?"

"Yes. I hear myself every time I try to not ask you to marry me and this time I ignored me because that me didn't see how much I don't want you to ever, for a second, believe you're anything other than my whole world."

Her eyes glisten with unshed tears, but the smile I'm waiting for doesn't come. A tear seeps out of the corner of each eye and she presses her lips together in an attempt to stop herself from crying. Releasing her neck, I pull her to my chest and hold her tight against me as she gathers my shirt in her fists.

"I ... don't ... know how ... to do this," she says between sobs.

I hold her tighter.

"It's okay. I don't know how to do this either. Isn't it great to learn how to do it together, though?"

124

"You're such a good guy, Damian. I'm such a screw up and I don't know why you'd even want to be with me," she says into my shirt.

We stand together silently in the kitchen as I carefully trail my fingers down her back and then up her neck. Massaging small circles along her shoulders until I feel her relax against me and the sniffles come farther apart, I wait for her to be ready to unpack this a little bit.

"You know I've never once thought you're a screw up. You chose a path that was a little more difficult, but you didn't screw up," I say.

Kissing the top of her head, I wait for her to respond. When she doesn't, I tip her chin up to look at her closely.

"He did a number on you while you were pregnant with Avery," I say. Watching her swallow hard is all the confirmation I need, but the wide eyes just double confirm it. "I'm not him. I love everything about you. Your curves. Your mood swings. Your cravings. The way you steal the covers so you can throw them off you as soon as you get too warm. I love pampering you and Avery through each stage of this part of our life together. I'm not leaving you, I'm not giving up on you, and I sure as hell am not going to treat you like you're less because the physical parts of you have changed."

Fresh tears blur her vision and she blinks them away.

"But what if—"

"What if I fall more in love with you by the time this kid gets here? That's a great question. I guess that's just what happens then," I say, shrugging. "We are going to live every moment together like it's the best one, even if it's not great. Because we communicate. Isn't that what they say? The key to a good relationship is communication."

She nods.

"We do. We communicate really well, usually," she says.

"So, what's happening here?"

"I haven't told you all of the things I'm afraid of and they built up and now, sometimes, I feel like you aren't going to love me once the baby is born because you'll have the baby to love and not need me because I'll be separate from the baby and it's stupid. It's stupid, Damian."

Smiling at her, I tip my head slightly and really get a good look at her.

"It is stupid," I say. She lightly smacks my chest, but cracks the slightest smile. "It's stupid because my love is not finite and if anything, I'm going to love you more after seeing you bring this person into the world. Then, after

125

you do that, I'm going to have three people who get infinite amounts of my love. Avery is really going to rock this big sister thing, don't you think?"

"She is. When you work late and I snuggle with her, she always curls up and talks to my belly," Elise says, but I already knew that's what happens. Avery tells me how she has full blown conversations with the belly. "Aves thinks the baby is a boy. Are you sure you don't want to find out?"

"Positive. I like the suspense."

I tip my forehead against Elise's, then place the tip of my nose on hers.

"I love you forever, Leesy. Forever and always."

"You haven't called me that since we were kids," she says, closing her eyes. A smile forms on her lips, a real smile that shows me she's content and at peace. "I love you forever and always, too."

*****

"You need to chill with the baby shower stuff, please. We don't need anything big and I really would like you to stop trying to invite people who hardly know me and Elise. It's not going well over here," I grumble into the phone, hoping my sister is actually listening on the other end.

"What happened?" she asks. I sense she's distracted, but can't be certain because she's in Buffalo and I am not, and she always seems to multitask when we're on the phone. "Elise hasn't said anything to me about the shower, so I assumed everything was fine."

It's a difficult ask, so I attempt to say it as gently as I can. Schooling my tone to be a little more sing-songy like when I'm convincing Avery to get out of bed in the morning for school, I go ahead and say what needs to be said.

"That's where you would be wrong. Have you talked to her about how she feels about the shower? Or have you just gone full bore, bull in a China shop, making plans?" Deep breath in, and release. "Because it feels like you're just making plans and trying to keep yourself busy instead of talking to us about things. With the exception of themes and color schemes, you haven't wanted a lot of input, Ang. You've just done what you want ..."

She's so quiet when I finish, I look at the phone to make sure we're still connected. I give it about thirty seconds before I clear my throat.

"Oh." She says it, but it's barely audible. "I ... I'm figuring out a place to have it, possibly the fire hall. They have a nice room with a fireplace that would be beautiful for photos."

"Don't ignore me, Angela."

"What do you want me to do? I'm trying to be helpful. My best friend is pregnant with my brother's baby, but it isn't her baby, and I'm not even local anymore so I have no idea what I'm supposed to be doing to help so I'm doing my best, Damian!" I let her have that. She's freaking out still about being far away from home. That's not a good enough excuse for ignoring what we're asking of her, which was nothing. Literally nothing. We weren't even going to have a baby shower. "I'm doing my best."

"I know you are. Now, I need you to stop trying so hard. I'm emailing you a new invite list. We're going to do this at my house because it's comfortable. Do not have it catered. Mac is in charge of food," I say, glad Elise and I had the conversation this morning about what we would actually want if Angela insisted on hosting this shindig. "You are fully in charge of the cake. Make it yourself, hire a baker, buy it from a grocery store … we don't care where it comes from. That's the biggest thing left that we want you to worry about."

Growing up, Angela tended to take on more than she could feasibly handle and when the emotional breakdown came, we all suffered for it. Through the years, I figured out how to mitigate the issues by leaving her with things she could control and addressing the rest of it, whatever it was. She still hasn't learned how to manage things when she attempts to split herself into multiple people.

"But what about the decorations?"

"We'll figure that out as we get closer, but right now I just want you to focus on the list I'm sending you and the cake," I say.

Putting me on speakerphone, I hear her set the phone down and then blow her nose.

"Thanks for not doing that in my ear, weirdo," I yell over the noise she's making.

"Are you going to tell me what happened?" she asks between blowing her nose. "You said it wasn't going well at your house."

I blow out a breath and massage my forehead.

"Well. It's been a lot of wondering how things will play out."

"More detail is necessary, Damian," she says, then takes me off speaker before yelling in my ear, "How what will play out?"

"She's just worried about her role with the baby as far as parenting goes. A little panicking about if she's still lovable," I say, trying not to go too deep into it since I know for a fact my sister will hang up with me and call Elise to find out what's going on if I don't play my cards right.

"She's not wrong to worry," she says.

"I know. She's in a precarious position, emotionally speaking, because it's unlike any of the surrogate stories we've read about through this whole thing," I say.

We're both quiet — me because I'm still worrying that Elise is worrying, Angela because she's likely plotting my demise for putting Elise in this situation. But would it have been any different if Elise and I had started dating and we got pregnant on our own together? When I really think about it, I think this outcome was going to happen eventually regardless, we just jumped straight to baby-making instead of dating first.

"She'll be fine. Elise is strong and you're a good partner for her, Damian. There's nothing you can say that's going to make me think you two aren't working through all of this together," Angela says. "You're the best guy for her."

I feel the same way. I just hope Elise does, too.

Chapter 19

ELISE

"Hey. What's going on? Damian said things have been difficult lately."

Not even a hello. I roll my eyes then immediately wonder why I'm irritated. She's my best friend. If I was dating anyone else, I would have called and talked to her about all my emotions. But since it's her brother? I've dodged texts and phone calls for three days. She finally got me on the line because she called from her work phone and I didn't recognize the number. I was hoping to yell at someone and let them know I am not worried about my car's extended warranty.

"Aren't you supposed to be working? It's," I pause, looking at the clock on the dash of my car before scrunching my nose, "it's not even eight in the morning. Why are you at work?"

"Honest? Because I knew you wouldn't answer the phone on your way to work if you saw it was my number and I want to know why."

"There's no reason. I'm just overwhelmed with things lately," I say, pulling up to a red light.

"Hmm I don't believe you," she says. "You know, I don't care that your guy is my brother. I'm still right here for you for always just like I have been the rest of our lives. Just ... don't tell me about the sex. Ew. That's ... ew."

I slowly accelerate when the light turns green, looking both ways before entering the intersection to make sure it's really clear. Saying nothing gives her more time to reload her thoughts.

"Anyway, I miss you and wanted to talk about the shower. Damian said you guys have food and location figured out, he sent me the new guest list, and put me in charge of the cake," she says.

I audibly sigh, a thankful sigh. Because I am thankful she's not jumping right back into things being difficult. Damain said he talked to her after my meltdown about who I am to this baby and all of the people on her original list. I expected her to want to talk to me about it. She's going to, in a roundabout way and I know that, so perhaps it would be easier to cut to the chase, but I'd rather not.

"What were you thinking for cake?"

"Well, you know how you told me to take detours and stuff when I come home and then back to Buffalo? I did. I went through Brockport, found a fabulous coffee shop and there's a bakery practically next door."

Her voice rises with excitement, and I feel my own mood lift. I'm talking to my best friend and it feels normal for the first time in weeks.

"And if you are up for it, maybe we could meet there and do a little cake tasting. Or not. I know it's a long drive, so I could just pick up tasting cakes and bring them home for us to sample. The baker said she could do either. It's up to you," Angela says.

"Really? You'd do that with me? Damian gave you all the decision-making power on the cake, so I don't want to step on your toes. I know cake is a very serious thing for you."

"I wouldn't ask you if I didn't want you to be part of it. How about I call Delilah and ask her to make me a sampler and I'll come home this weekend for a little private taste testing?"

I'm surprised, but also not, because Angela will find any reason she can to come home for a weekend or a long weekend or anything that resembles a break.

"That sounds fantastic. Is there anything I can do to make this a little more fancy than just sitting around eating cake?" I ask as I pull into the parking lot at work. "Mocktails? Fruit platter?"

Angela lets out a laugh and it feels so good to not be weird with one another.

"No, I don't want you to lift a finger. Let's just chill and eat cake and hang out," she says, but there's a heaviness in the air. Then she adds, "Like we used to."

*****

"So, she says, 'like we used to,' and now I feel like a shitty friend. Damian, I've become that friend who pulls away when things change. I don't want to be that friend," I say at the end of telling him about my conversation with his sister. "How do I fix this?"

Pushing another spoonful of chicken salad into my mouth, I wait for him to respond and try to not crunch celery in his ear.

"I think you are fixing it. Just do the best friend stuff you guys have always done. Avery and I will stay out of the way. I'm designing a new playroom for a client, so I need her input anyway," he says. "It will be good for all of you."

"What do you mean?" I ask, because I'm genuinely curious. My brain is mush lately and maybe I missed something else that I need to fix.

"I mean, this is the first time ever you and Angela have lived this far apart and I know it's killing you that she's not here for every little thing. Not just the baby, but everything. Avery's Halloween parade at school? That's a thing Ang would have normally been at. Every end of a bad week at school for you? Ang would have been over for a bitch session with you until you both felt better. Angela is also used to you being there for everything with her. You both need this, and Avery needs this, and honestly ... I miss my sister, too," he says.

Damian is so laid back about his sister, I haven't really contemplated how he's dealing with her living so far away. We've both tried to make Angela see it's not as bad as it could be, but maybe it is. Maybe it is as bad as she makes it out to be. Maybe the distance between us is more than we can handle.

"I want her to move closer to home."

"Me, too. But we can't tell her that," he says quickly. "Mostly because she'll just quit and move home. We don't want her to give up her dreams and Mac already told her she's not allowed to come work for him again."

We both laugh about it, but Mac was dead serious.

"This weekend, you'll taste the delicious cakes from this little bakery my sister found. You and Angela will decide the best one and she'll handle the order," he says, getting back on track. "You'll both unload all your emotional burdens and work through things like you always do. Then on Sunday, I'll make breakfast and everything will be normal again."

"Normal." I let out a tight laugh at the end of the statement. "I don't know if normal will ever define any of us ever again."

"Noted," he says. "Don't you have children you're supposed to be teaching? Lunch is over, Leesy."

"Crap, yes!" I say, grabbing my lunch bag and ending the call after a quick, "Love you."

Tossing my stuff in my cubby, I beeline for my classroom. From the door I watch Julia get our afternoon class situated. Boots are put on the shoe rack and jackets hung up, hands are sanitized, and like clockwork each little body finds its way to a chair.

Julia turns and sees me watching, offering a small smile.

"Thank you. I lost track of time dealing with some personal business," I say.

"I figured this part is easy enough. If you weren't back from lunch by the time they were settled, I would have asked Laura to get you," she says, quietly. "Everything okay?"

Nodding, because I hope to move beyond this quickly, I begin taking attendance.

"Okay, because it sounded like you were dealing with some drama," Julia says, almost as if she didn't think through what was coming out of her mouth.

I stop what I'm doing, my pen poised in the air.

"No drama," I say, lifting my head up to look at her. "There is no drama. I know you mean well, but please don't make assumptions based on a snippet of a conversation you overheard. Hopefully, overheard accidentally and didn't eavesdrop on since that would be rude and unkind and very unbecoming of a person who works with children."

My voice is calm and the words come out fast. I realize I used the teacher voice on her when Julia's eyes widen and her jaw drops.

"No, Elise. I swear, I mean nothing malicious. Your voice carried a bit and you sounded stressed about whatever you were talking about," she says, stuttering through her explanation.

Julia looks mortified I would think she was eavesdropping on my conversation with Damian. Sadly, I can't believe she wasn't. It's how too many other co-workers behave and if any of them actually knew there was something slightly askew with my life situation it would be like feeding myself to the wolves. I choose to not be dinner.

"Please know I respect the hell out of you," she says, lowering her voice. "And truly admire how hard you work, here and with your own daughter, because not everyone is that dedicated. I just don't want to see you have bad days. If anyone deserves good days, it's you."

I'm flabbergasted, because she means it. I swallow the thickness in my throat as I thank her and do my best to hide my face as I wipe the errant tears before they slip down my face.

"That means a lot to me. Sometimes, it's hard to feel appreciated here," I say.

She nods, understanding because most of the rest of the staff hasn't always shown their best sides. Julia has shared with me that the few times she went out for drinks with other people, conversations centered around who they didn't like at work, which parents of students they disliked the most, and some very X-rated themes about some dads. None of the times she went did they care that she's brand new and my teaching assistant and they tended to talk shit about me. Fun times.

Allowing myself to show emotion with Julia has taken time. When she was first hired, she was trying to make friends. I was unsure how much trust to put into her as an acquaintance knowing how others here can be. But she didn't grow up here and only landed in this town because of a guy who turned out to be not all that great. Her story is starting to sound like mine, but without a preschooler in tow.

Taking a long look at Julia, I make a decision. One Angela is just going to have to deal with.

"Are you free Saturday?"

*****

"'Sup?" she says when she answers halfway through the first ring.

"I did a thing and I know you might be upset, but I need you to handle your emotions," I say, as I pull out of the parking lot.

"That sounds … ominous."

"For you, it might be. Saturday," I say.

Before I can fully form or complete my thought, Angela says, "Are you cancelling on me?"

"Absolutely not. I'm making it more fun. I hope," I say. She gives me an "uh huh" so I continue. "I invited Julia over to hang out. She's attempted to hang with the wrong girls here and I think she's just looking for something normal. Like us."

Silence. Okay, I tell myself, it's not that bad. She hasn't balked at the idea and she didn't hang up on me.

"The girl who isn't taking my place?"

"Yes, her. And she still isn't taking your place. We're collectively opening our arms to welcome a new person to tentatively join the coven. If we were witches. You know how it is," I say, rambling like a pro.

My heart feels lighter when I hear her laughter through the line.

133

"You're ridiculous, you know that, right?"

"Your brother tells me that all the time. So, is this okay?"

I give her a minute to think it over and when she still hasn't said anything I ask if I lost her.

"No, I'm still here," she says. "I think ... this will be great. I'd like to meet her."

"You know you're the best, right Ang? This is a lot for me to ask of you, but it's a lot for me to work at a place where I don't have friends," I say. "At the diner, I have our regulars and I have Mac. The school? I keep my distance from pretty much everyone and always have. I work well with them, but friendships outside of work? I've been really good about staying out of the insanity, and they still find things about me to talk about behind my back."

"I know, Lise. I know," she says. "Listen, I've got to run. There's a staff meeting and I'm already a little behind. I'll talk to you soon. I love you."

"Love you, too, Ang."

Hanging up the call as I pull into the driveway, I sit in my parked car until the tears stop. This week has just been too much for my emotions. They just keep coming, until I hear the passenger door open and quickly wipe my face. Checking myself in the mirror first, I turn to Damian. Holding onto the roof of the car and the open door, he bends his upper body so he can look in on me.

"Do you realize you've been sitting out here, in the cold no less, for the length of three Bluey episodes? Three, Elise."

The serious set to his jaw, how it ticks slightly at the end of his comment, and the way his eyes bore into me, catch me off-guard. I'm used to gentle Damian. He's the warmth I wrap myself up in each night. I'm not sure if I want to cry more or have him ravage me in the backseat. Maybe both.

"How many?" I ask, watching for any other clues that he's upset with me or just messing with me.

"Three," he says, slowly. "Are you coming in the house with me? You look like you need a mug of cocoa and a blanket, and probably an orgasm or two."

Without trying, I let out a sigh because, "Yes. All of those sound perfect. I'm just not sure if I can get out of my seat."

He doesn't say another word as he closes the passenger door and walks around the front of the car to open mine. Reaching in over the top of my ever-expanding belly, he unbuckles my seatbelt, then releases the steering wheel so it's up as far as it goes.

"What ..." I start and stop. "Wait, what are you doing?"

He slides one arm behind my back and the other under my legs, then pulls me from the car.

"You realize how much I weigh, right? I'm not a small girl right now, Damian. You're going to hurt your back," I say, laughing, though I'm definitely worried he'll drop me. "This baby is making me fat."

He stops in his tracks halfway to the house.

"I love you, so don't take this the wrong way, but that's the dumbest thing I have ever heard you say," he remarks. "You're growing a human being. You're not fat. And even if you were? I would never in a thousand years think that or say that."

Overly emotional. Unable to control my emotions. Super sensitive. Call it whatever you want.

I start crying again and wrap my arms around his neck.

"It was a long day," I say. "Can we do take out and snuggle with Avery until bedtime? I missed her a lot today."

"As you wish."

M.L. PENNOCK

Chapter 20

DAMIAN

She's been off kilter all week. It started with the baby shower invitations. Then, ongoing coworker issues since they all want to talk shit non-stop about everyone else in the building — but not Julia, because apparently she's pretty cool and Elise is warming up to the idea of having a friend at work who has a little more insider information that anyone else ever has. Tanner called late Thursday, around bedtime for Avery, and that put us all in a funk after not hearing from him for months. Elise has done what she can to remain in contact with his family for Avery's sake, but has all but written Tanner off as a "phone call on your birthday" father.

Now that Friday is here, you'd think we could just relax a little, but that's not life lately. After school, Avery had a snack and we decided to get right to work.

"Okay, Aves, so I need you to tell me all the things you would want in a playroom."

"Like, anything at all?"

"Anything goes. We just need to start brainstorming for my client. He's got a couple kids who are super active and needs us to design a jungle gym for inside his house," I say, pulling out colored pencils and graph paper.

"Can we build one of those here for me and my baby?" she asks, drawing a circle on her paper.

"Well, the baby wouldn't be able to play on something like that for quite a while. But, what about a swing? Do you think a swing would work well inside?"

Shrugging, she taps her pencil against her bottom lip.

"Maaaaaybe. My school has one that's like a cocoon. How 'bout that?"

"Perfect," I say, writing it in my notes as my mind starts forming a picture of what this design will look like when it's completed.

Working with a little kid on a project for little kids is the smartest thing I've done in a while. She hasn't lost her creativity or sense of wonder, so everything sounds like a good idea. Right down to the rock wall.

I need to know if it would work. Getting up from the worktable in my office where Avery and I have made ourselves at home for the night, I grab my tape measure and leave the room.

"Wait for me! I'm working, too!" Avery yells as she comes barreling out of the office hot on my heels. "Where we going, D?"

"Basement," I say, looking at my little shadow and winking. "I have an idea."

We measure, and measure again, and my brain feels like it's on fire. This could work. Then, I'd also have a working model to promote.

"Yeah, Aves. I think we might be able to build one for you and your baby," I say, pulling the pencil from behind my ear and writing the last measurement on the wall of my unfinished basement.

I can't believe I never thought about using this space for the kids. I mean, up until last year there were no "kids" and now ... there are kids. I just figured it would be mostly storage, but this is a way better idea.

"Damian?" Elise calls from the top of the stairs. "Are you down there?"

"Yeah, we are. Come here, I want to talk to you about something," I holler back up.

Hearing a chair slide across the floor above me, I wait for Angela and Elise to make their way down the stairs. Before they even touch the last step, I'm talking to them about the project I'm designing for my client. Avery, the little sales person that she is, pipes up with her ideas for having something similar at home. My sister and girlfriend watch with amused looks as Avery and I talk non-stop about jungle gyms and slides and climbing apparatuses and cocoon swings.

"I thought you wanted this to be a home gym?" Angela says, covering her smirk.

"Yes, initially that was my plan, but then it just didn't happen and it became a little bit storage and whole lot of unused space," I say. Placing my hands on my hips, I look down at Avery beside me and she looks up at me. "I like this idea better."

"Me too," she says, nodding her head matter-of-factly. "Then me and my baby can play all year long even when it's rainin' and snowin'. We haven't played on the playground at school in forever because of mud."

"What's wrong with mud?" Angela asks, poking the bear.

"Nothin'. But at school they don't want me dirty. At home, I'm allowed."

"Fair," Elise says. Turning her attention back to me, she says, "So, we're building an indoor play center for our kids now? Is that what you're saying?"

"I do believe that's what we're talking about," I respond, with a crooked grin. "Don't tell me you don't love the idea. I see the sparkle in your eye, Leesy."

She pulls the edge of her bottom lip in between her teeth, pretending to mull it over before shrugging.

"Yeah, I do. But it's going to cost a fortune," she says.

"Probably. Good thing I have a fortune saved up," I say, shrugging right back.

I don't want her worrying about the money. She knows that's not something I want her worrying about. She even argued with me about still giving her money for carrying the baby, but that's a contractual agreement and just because she sleeps in our bed and lives at our house now wasn't a reason to break the contract and not provide her with what she needs and agreed to. That's honestly an argument I never in a thousand years thought I would have with anyone.

"Okay," she says, quietly. "I guess we're going to build a playground in the basement. Can Angela and I go back upstairs now? You and Avery have your work cut out for you."

I saunter toward her, looking directly into her eyes until the space between us is minimal.

"Aves. Let's go upstairs. Let Mom and Damian talk for a minute," Angela says from beside me.

Out of the corner of my eye I watch as she takes Avery's hand and leads her back up the stairs to the main floor of the house. Once they're gone, my eyes drop to Elise's lips. Ever so slowly, she tucks her bottom lip in between her teeth again. In all the years I've known her, nibbling on her bottom lip has always been a nervous habit, one I secretly love because I know how to make her stop.

Placing my thumb carefully against the divot above her chin, I grasp her jaw and pull her lip from her mouth. Her eyes widen, her pupils dilate slightly, and I fall a little harder.

"You're part of the decision making," I say.

"I ... I know. It just sometimes feels like my input isn't needed," she says, shyly.

"That's just it. Your input is necessary. Your input is what keeps me grounded. Are you sure you're okay with this project? It literally just came out of nowhere. Avery wondered if we could do one here since we're designing one for my client and I needed to explore the option, see if we had the space down here," I say, sliding my palm to rest on the side of her neck. "If you think it's something we should wait with, we'll wait. If you think it's something you want to research more, we'll do it. I'm not building this in my house."

"But you are. It is your house."

"No. It's our house, Elise. Ours. You and I share it. This is our home."

"But the money. This is going to cost so much money."

"It's just money. I'll make more next month. The client I'm designing this project for? The cost to him alone will more than cover the cost for our project. Why are you worrying about money?"

"Because. We didn't grow up with a lot, Damian. I always worry about money. I always live like it's scarce. I always shop for the best prices because I don't want to pay more for something if I don't have to because I've never had more," she says. "You've … you've built this amazing life for you and welcomed me and Avery into it like we won't make you go broke if we get used to living this life, too. And I'm scared it's all just going to disappear."

Pulling her close to me, I wrap my arms around her shoulders and tuck her head under my chin.

"We can't live like that. I don't want you to live in fear of having nothing," I say. "And I don't want my daughter and my new baby to grow up believing they aren't worth everything. They are."

"Your daughter?" she questions.

"She's practically mine. It's just semantics. When she's out with me in town, people who don't know Tanner, know Avery is mine. Sometimes, even people who know Tanner is her father treat me like I'm her only dad."

Her arms pull me tighter to her, as close as we can get with the small basketball hidden away beneath her shirt, and we hold one another.

"I need you to hug me like this more," she says into the fabric covering my chest. "I need you to need me like I need you."

"I do. I always have. It's always been you, Elise. Always."

*****

140

The project has been greenlit by all the women in the house, including the one who doesn't live here, so Avery and I made a more inclusive list of what could potentially be included in the build. That list will be one my client can pick and choose from since he seemed to be unsure what he wanted. If it weren't for Avery, there are a lot of things I might not have thought to include, like cargo nets. I loved cargo nets as a kid, but I've forgotten about some of the coolest stuff after being an adult for so long.

Once everyone was on board, I sent my sister and Elise out for a girl's night. I wanted them to go get something to eat and just act like the almost 30-year-olds they are, because they haven't been able to do that and tomorrow, they've invited Julia over. This gives them the time together they desperately need.

Avery got through a bath with extra time to soak in her bubbles before rinsing and getting all the extra soap off. I learned my lesson the hard way with not having her rinse really well. While it was a great learning experience for me, it was a lot of itchy skin for Avery and I never want to deal with that again if I can prevent it. I filed the information away in my brain so I don't make the same mistake twice.

Pajamas on, popcorn popped, and a movie ended our work day.

I'm carrying her to her room when I hear the door open and the girls come in. They're tiptoeing around the kitchen when I come back from tucking Avery in and start picking up the blankets from a fort we made halfway through the movie and stack the cups and bowls from snacks.

"You need to tell him," I overhear my sister say somewhat loudly. "Have you told him?"

I don't mean to listen, but I don't back away from the doorway either.

"We talked about it. My brain just can't decide if it's in agreement with my heart. Plus, what if he does change his mind, Angela? What if he doesn't want a family, he just wants the baby? Avery and I … we're a lot," Elise says.

I thought we'd figured this out? I thought she was okay?

"I'm a walking incubator and falling in love with this little person I'm growing, but what if Damian doesn't want me to be their mom? That's the part that's going to kill me," she says.

"Has he said anything to make you think he doesn't want that?"

Elise let's out an unironic laugh, followed by a deep sigh.

"Just the opposite. He's all but proposed," she says, and I smile. "It's me. I'm the problem."

"So quit being the fucking problem and become my sister-in-law. Let's get you two hitched and then the next baby can be a you and Damian creation instead of baby a la test tube," Angela says. I almost walk into the kitchen after that to defend my unborn child, but stop short when she continues talking. "I love my littlest niece or nephew and you are the best person to grow them. Damian? That guy doesn't give up his heart easily, Elise. He hid his feelings for you for years, I'm finding out, and yours for him. The two of you are right for one another. Everything you're freaking out about? That's your insecurity talking."

I don't breathe. This doesn't sound like the same sister who threatened my life if I hurt her best friend.

"He's. Not. Tanner. Repeat after me. He's not Tanner. He's not going to make you do this alone. He's not going to steal money from you. He's not going to decide he doesn't want to be a father when it gets too hard," Angela says. "He's in it for forever and you and I both know it. Maybe he's using all the right words and just not putting them in the correct order, but you're his entire world and you're making his dreams come true. I know my big brother. He wouldn't have chosen you to spend his life with if you weren't made for him. He's extremely picky in this regard."

Barely audible, I hear Elise say, "I just don't want to let him down."

"You won't," I say, forgetting I'm not part of this conversation when I hear both of them gasp. "Shit."

"Dude. Being creepy in your own house? It's not even Halloween," Angela says.

I take the few steps from the living room into the kitchen. There is no denying I was listening to their conversation, but there's also no reason for me to not be part of it. Elise and I have talked about all of this and if she needed to hear from my sister — from her best friend — that we're going to make it, then so be it. That's why a girl's night was necessary.

"You won't. You won't let me down. We're partners in this, in everything. I may be oblivious to a lot of what you're feeling, I know what we're doing is unconventional, but that doesn't mean I love you any less," I say. "I want to marry you. I want you to help me raise this baby."

"But legally —"

"I looked into it. You can be on the birth certificate. It might be a little more complicated than that, but I want you on the birth certificate," I say emphatically. "I want you to be this baby's mother. You already are, Elise."

"But what about what I want?" she says, pointing to herself. "You just said a lot of 'I want' and didn't ask if that's what I want, too."

I blink. I look at my sister. Did I fucking miss something? Angela's looking between us like she's watching a tennis match. Then I look back at Elise and know what she's doing.

"Elise," I say, stepping closer to her. "Look me in the eyes. I know I can be kind of selfish. We both can be. That's because we're human. No one is completely selfless all the time. I need to know what you want because we're either all in or not at all. You can play devil's advocate all you want, but it's not going to change the fact you want this baby as much as I do and plan to be here with us through thick and thin."

"I know. But I want you to know that it requires a lot of give and take. You want me on the birth certificate. Fabulous. I want that, too. But did you ask me if that's what I wanted? Because we didn't have a conversation about it, and that's a big deal," she says, calmly.

The serene tone she uses is what makes her the perfect teacher. She schools me every chance she can, even on her hardest weeks, because when I'm wrong, I'm wrong.

"No. We didn't and it was wrong of me to assume instead of ask," I say, handing the dirty dishes in my arms to my sister and grabbing Elise's hands. "Elise, I am madly in love with you and I am hoping you will do me the honor of being my child's other parent, legally and in every other way. Will you please be my baby's mama?"

A smile cracks her otherwise concrete façade. Before I know it, she's beaming, then laughing, and finally wrapped up in my arms where she belongs.

"I hate when you make me second guess everything," I say against her neck.

"I know, but you need to remember you don't speak for me. I went through hell with the last guy and, even though I'm usually timid with you and let you have your way, I'll stand my ground when I have to," she says.

"You didn't answer his question," Angela says from her spot near the sink, a glass of water in her hand. When we both look at her curiously, she says, "What? I was listening. You didn't answer his question. I mean, it's not the question I was hoping he was going to ask, but still."

Elise looks back at me, down at her belly, then at me again.

"Yes."

Chapter 21

ELISE

Saying yes to something never felt so right.

Standing at the doors to the deck, I trail my fingers down my belly, cupping my hands beneath the bump and cradling it gently, knowing in the coming months it will grow to potentially painful proportions. Watching inky darkness slowly fade as the sun comes up behind the house, the trees that line the lake being lit on fire with the warmth of a winter sunrise, I take in the silence of ... home. The quiet — just me and this baby — is the best time to not think. I just feel. I let it wash over me, coming in waves as I work through the last few years.

I've gone through a lot of hurt. Tanner messed with my mind in ways no one else ever had, and even though it might not be the worst by some people's standards, it was by mine. He lied to me. He stole from me. He took money, years, and freedom. He broke promises. He made every moment with him hurt, and then for reasons I can't comprehend, I didn't want to let him go. For the longest time I held on and just ... couldn't let him go. I tried to make him live up to the reputation he had of being a nice guy. I spent years not listening to the people who really knew him, ignoring the red flags Mac showed me in favor of the green ones his mother shared.

Until Ang. It wasn't until Angela took me out one night and talked to me about all the ways I'm worth more. I deserve more. My daughter deserves more.

Now we have more. But I still struggle to see my worth in Damian's world, and he's the biggest green flag guy I have ever known. I won't lie to myself and say all the hurt wasn't worth it. I have Avery and she alone, the two of us coming out on the other side of my relationship with her father, was worth us moving through it. We're both a little more free to be ourselves these days and the weight of my insecurities is lighter after last night. I get to have my family grow and as a little foot kicks me from the inside, I smile. Loving this baby is one of my favorite parts of life. I don't have to hide it, I don't have to pretend this child isn't part of me and Avery, because even without being connected by blood we're family. Being asked to be his or her mother? It's the best question he could have asked me in this moment in time.

Damian has told me time and again his love is not finite, and I'm finally believing him. It's taken me a while to get here, but I needed to truly understand what family means to me. Angela, Mac, Damian ... they're my family, and they love me more than Tanner ever could, because Tanner loves himself most.

When my phone lights up with an incoming call before the sun is fully above the horizon, my immediate reaction is fear. Fear something happened to my parents, or Angela, or Damian and Ang's parents. Because fear always follows my happiness. I never thought I would hear his voice, as if just the thought of him conjured his presence out of the abyss.

"Hey, I got myself into some trouble," Tanner says.

"Trouble? In Austin?" I scoff.

"There was a fight at the bar," he begins.

One of the bands he's managing was playing at a local bar. There were rowdy customers in all states of drunkenness. He'd been drinking, too, he says. It's the same story, just a different part of the country this time.

"What are they charging you with?" I ask once he's done explaining how he's innocent in all of this.

"Assault ... with a deadly weapon," he says, adding that he knocked a man unconscious with a bar stool. He's quiet, waiting for me to respond, but I can't. "So aggravated assault, I guess. Listen, can you bail me out or not? You've got extra money now that you're pregnant with that baby for Damian. I know you have enough."

The guy he hit is in the hospital. My ex is in jail, where he belongs. Where he should have been a long time ago. Whether I have enough money to do anything is none of his business. He is no longer my problem.

"No," I say.

"What? You're joking right?"

"No. It's a complete sentence. It's a sentence I have never said to you, but you need to get used to hearing it now," I say, shaking as the adrenaline courses through my veins and my heartrate skyrockets. "Call your parents. I'm not your piggy bank."

I don't pay attention to what he says beyond that and pull the phone from my ear. I know he's angry. I know he's probably hurting. Now, he's going to have to deal with the consequences of the issues he has created.

Staring at the trees across the lake, I hope whatever repercussion he's dealt will teach him the lessons he so desperately needs to learn. Living in his hometown for as long as he did certainly didn't do him any favors.

I feel Damian come up behind me before I hear him. The way his energy surrounds me before he ever touches me should be calming, but instead? I fall apart. All he had to do was touch my shoulders and the sobbing started. As Damian comes to stand in front of me and collects me into his arms, I let everything go. All the hurt and hate and healing I haven't done.

"What happened?"

Catching my breath, I say, "Tanner. Tanner happened."

He gives me another moment to pull myself together, and then I tell him. I tell him everything. It's years of shit I haven't shared with anyone but Angela and I try to give Damian the cliff's notes version. "Try" being the operative word, because as I'm talking and the stories are getting longer, he leads me to the kitchen to start the coffee maker. As if we've been doing this for our entire adult lives, I pull out flour and milk and eggs to start a batch of pancakes. We don't skip a beat and he asks all the questions he needs to.

As the coffee finishes brewing, a cup is poured and set beside me while I continue talking and flipping breakfast over on the griddle.

"His lack of ability to be an adult makes me hurt. I hurt for my daughter, Damian. Eventually, she's going to ask why Daddy can't visit. How do you explain to your little girl her father hurt someone so badly he's going to sit in jail? Because, for the record, I hope he's going to be in jail for a while."

"Well, I think when she asks, you be as honest as you can for her age," Damian says. "That's all you can do. Tanner hurt someone and he's in trouble. He's going to have to do his time. If the charges hold, he's now got a felony on his record, right?"

"I know," I say, quietly coming to terms that he's right. I need to be honest with her about this, but probably not until she asks about him.

"She's not mine, legally, but I don't think I want him around her when he gets out. Not alone," Damian says, leaning against the counter while he sips his coffee. "I know he would never do anything to hurt her when he's sober. I just don't know if I want to trust him with her at all."

I don't disagree. I don't fully agree with him either. I'm just taking it all in because this has been a little too much too early in the morning.

"Let's just let it play out how it's supposed to. You told him you aren't bailing him out, and even if you did, he wouldn't be able to leave Texas because he'll have court dates. It's a felony. It's not going to go away ... and if something else happens to the guy he assaulted, then they could tack on more charges," he says.

He's just thinking out loud, I can tell by the monotone cadence to his voice that he's not talking to me, but he's right. If the man he put in the hospital dies from his injuries? That's a worse outcome for Tanner.

"Can we stop talking about this for now? I can't manage regular emotions with pregnancy emotions on a normal day, and now I have extra big emotions on top of both of those," I say.

Damian nods and leans into me, kissing my temple and picking up my cup to give me a splash more of hot coffee since mine has grown lukewarm. As he hands it back to me, we hear Avery coming through the living room.

"Hey, Sunshine! Guess what today is?" Damian says to her, switching gears just like I need him to.

"Cake tasting day with Aunt Ang!" she yells, running to him while clutching her elephant.

"Yes, ma'am, it is. Do you think Mommy is going to let me try them, too?" he asks, scooping her up.

Avery shrugs. "Maybe if you're a good boy, she'll let you."

I laugh because that one little phrase triggers in me the memory of saying that to him once and the way his body responded, the way his eyes looked after I pulled away from him. It seems like a lifetime ago, but really, it was the beginning of the life we are making.

"Yeah, Damian. Maybe if you're a good boy I'll let you taste the cake," I say, smirking as I place the jug of maple syrup and a stack of plates on the table.

He catches my eye and sets Avery down in a chair.

"You are going to cause trouble if you keep talking like that," he says without breaking eye contact as he walks closer to me. "I'd love to taste your cake, though."

"Maybe Angela can come over earlier and take Avery to the park."

"It's January," he says in my ear. "And snowing."

"Grocery store." I hear the pleading in my voice and I'm almost sorry for it. Almost.

"Are you desperate?" he questions, as he lifts one eyebrow and his eyes trail toward the living room.

"I might be a little desperate. It's been a lot of emotions this morning and when those build up, they need to be released somehow," I say. "What time is Ang supposed to be here?"

"I'll text and tell her to get over here ASAP or she'll miss out on pancakes," he says. "Or … Aves, how about a show with breakfast?"

My eyes go wide as he whips his phone from his pocket, opens an app, and I hear the beginning of one of her current favorite shows. This isn't a normal routine for her. We limit screens at the table the best we can.

"Today is amazing!" Avery says as I quickly cut up another pancake for her.

"It sure is, baby girl," I say as Damian grabs my hand and pulls me away from the kitchen until we're practically running to the bedroom.

Calling out behind him, Damian adds, "Mom's gotta shower. We'll be back soon."

The door closes behind me and I hear him turn the lock.

"Maybe you aren't a good boy after all. This all feels a little naughty," I say.

As he turns me around to face him, his eyes darken and it makes the blood rush to my clit and begin to throb.

"You've never snuck away to handle business while she's busy?" he questions.

"Um, I haven't had anyone who wants to 'handle business' with me so it was a non-issue."

The way his eyes bore into me, knowing he knows every detail of how deprived I was before him, sends a shiver across my skin.

"If you don't hurry up, I'm going to have to take care of things myself," I say in a desperate plea.

"We can't have you doing that now can we?" he says rhetorically.

Reaching for my hand, he pulls me along as he steps toward the ensuite bathroom. Once through the door, he turns and grasps my face in his hands, angling my mouth in a way that suits him, and crashes his lips to mine. Kissing me furiously, I take everything he gives me and give back in return until my chest is heaving and his lips are swollen. Breaking away from me, he pushes my flannel pajama pants down my legs and then slowly releases each button on the matching top until my breasts are covered but my belly is bare and on full display. Sliding his hands along my abdomen, gently holding my protruding belly, he sinks to his knees and places tender kisses along the line leading from my belly button to my pelvis.

"I love this," he says, then kisses low on my belly again.

Trailing his fingers up my leg from the ankle until he reaches the apex of my thighs, he slowly works one finger into my core, saying, "And I love how wet you are for me."

Placing my hand on the counter for balance as he dips his head between my legs, I prepare myself for the onslaught of sensation. As he slowly flicks his tongue against the most sensitive part of my body, Damian bends my knee and places my thigh on his shoulder.

"That's better," he says, quickly diving back between my thighs.

I love a long lovemaking session, crave it most of the time, but this morning I'm so worked up that he's hardly touched me and I feel the beginnings of an orgasm building. He slips a second finger into me, massaging all the right spots, and before I can ask him to slow down, I'm tossing my head back and my legs begin to shake. Holding me up, Damian remains in his kneeling position until he's drawn the last shuddering wave from my body.

"Holy. Shit."

"That's got to be a record," he says, a low growling moan escaping his throat. "Do you think you have one more in you?"

Staring down at him, I smile.

"I'm willing to give it a try if you are," I say.

Pulling my leg from his shoulder and turning to face the counter, he understands exactly what I want. He drags his hands up the outsides of my legs as he comes to stand behind me. I twist enough to watch as he bends to nip the skin on my ass before doing the same to my lower back. When I turn back to face the mirror, he makes eye contact with me while unzipping his jeans and releasing his pulsing cock. Teasing me with just the head of his penis is too much, and I push back against him, slowly grinding into his pelvis until he takes his cock in his hand and guides it into me.

"Please," I say, when he stops and takes a deep breath.

"I love the way you feel around me," he says, reaching out to wrap his fingers in my hair. Tugging gently, always so gentle, he pulls my head back as he finishes entering me in one swift movement. "You're so tight. I'm not going to last long."

"I don't need you to last long. I just need you to come in me as quickly as possible," I blurt out.

As if that's the only thing he needed to hear, Damian slams his hips into me again and stops.

"Fuck," he says, grinding his teeth. "You're such a bossy woman."

"You love it. Please, fuck me. I need to feel your hard cock," I say.

He unwinds his fingers from my hair and places both hands on my hips as he begins rocking into me, each time hitting all the right parts and triggering the onslaught of another orgasm. I attempt to subdue my moans, but each one brings on another satisfied groan from Damian until I tighten my core around him and hear his breath hitch.

"You're going to make me come again. I'm so close," I say, reaching down between my legs to feel our connection and rub lazy circles on my clit. The pulsing grows stronger until I can't hold it any longer and my insides clench around him. "Oh my ... fuck."

"I'm ..." and he can't finish his statement as his hips connect once more with me. He holds onto me like a lifeline, leaning forward to kiss between my shoulder blades as his cock pulses deep within me.

Panting, attempting to catch my breath, I say, "I think I really do need a shower now."

Laughing, he kisses my back once more before finding the energy to pull out. "Same. I promise not to make you orgasm again if you let me jump in with you."

"Save water. Shower together. We need to hurry, though."

It doesn't take long for us to wash up and, as I rinse my hair, he steps out of the walk-in shower. Turning the water off, I squeeze the excess from my hair, and open my eyes just in time to catch him watching me through the glass. A towel is slung low on his hips and he looks every bit as delicious as he did when I was in high school trying to not want my best friend's older brother.

"I never thought the nerdy guy would get the hot girl," he says, wrapping a towel around my body as I step out of the shower. "Not only did I get you ... I get to keep you."

Holding the fabric to my chest, I lift up on my toes to kiss him.

"You're one lucky guy, you know that?" I say, not hiding my smile.

"I count the stars every night."

Chapter 22

DAMIAN

I dress quickly so Avery doesn't come looking for us. We snuck off for almost a half hour and I was surprised she didn't try to bust into the bedroom to find us before Elise had her first orgasm, let alone left us long enough for her to have a second. Without intent, I feel my back straighten and my chest puff out a bit knowing I did that for her. It might be a source of pride for the rest of the day and no one else is going to know it.

"Aves, how's your show?" I say, rolling my sleeve up my forearm as I walk through the living room.

Elise is taking time to dry her hair and put on a little makeup before Angela and Julia get here, so I'm tasked with getting Avery the rest of the way ready for the day.

"How was your shower?"

My head snaps up at the sound of my sister's voice.

"I thought you weren't coming over until noonish?"

"I got bored and wanted to hang out more. Avery said Elise was in the shower and since you weren't out here, I put the clues together," she says. "She only wanted to come tell you guys I was here half a dozen times and I convinced her to wait. You're welcome."

I feel the heat creep up my neck.

"Busted," Elise says behind me. "It is what it is. I had a rough morning and he was kind enough to help me work through some stuff."

Pouring myself a fresh cup of coffee, I listen as Elise tries to quietly share the news about Tanner with my sister.

"He's fucked. This, on top of whatever misdemeanors he has from up here, along with whatever drugs they probably found on him and I imagine they aren't going to go easy on him," Angela says. She must notice me staring at her, because she says, "You didn't know about the drugs?"

"He didn't know about the drugs," Elise says. "It was pot and pills usually, but I know after I kicked him out, he had gotten into other stuff. We're speculating about them finding something on him, though, and honestly, I don't care. I just don't want him thinking he's going to get to walk back in

153

here and have a relationship with our daughter after this. Figuratively walking in here. I wouldn't literally allow him within a hundred feet of the front door."

They've attempted to keep their voices as quiet as possible as we huddle near the coffee pot, but it's a difficult topic so as she's talking Elise's voice is slowly getting louder.

"Is there anything in particular you want Avery to wear today or just whatever?" I say, attempting to briefly change the topic while turning to look in Aves' general direction.

Elise understands exactly what I'm doing and instantly looks mortified.

"Whatever she wants to wear. Leggings, jeans, anything she's comfortable in. We'll be eating cake, so no need to dress her in anything fancy," she says, knowing full well I would put that child in first day of school clothes if the occasion called for it or Avery requested it.

"Jeans and T-shirt!" Avery yells as she shimmies out of the chair at the dining room table and takes off running toward her bedroom. "And no socks!"

"I guess that answers that," Elise says, laughing as I kiss her on the cheek before running off after Avery.

"Okay, kiddo, let's get you dressed and then you can play before Mommy kicks off this cake contest of hers," I say, stepping into Avery's room.

She's standing in her closet, pants and shirts strewn all over the floor amidst baby dolls and stuffed animals. My breath catches, watching as she picks up one pair of jeans and drops it on the floor in favor of a different one, and an image of an older Avery flashes in my head. I can't help but hope we'll still be spending time together like this when she's a teenager. She's been my movie watching partner and co-artist, and now helping with my actual fun work things, for as long as I can remember, but today is different and I don't like the feeling that she's going to grow up too fast. I know some of it is because of the trouble Tanner has gotten himself into. I don't want to think about the hurt she could be experiencing if she knew what was going on with him, and I know Elise and I will have a conversation with her about it eventually. Today, I just want to enjoy the fact I get to be her dad, even if I'm not her father.

"Damian, you aren't hearing me."

"What? No, I wasn't listening. What did I miss?" I ask coming out of my thoughts.

"I ... have nothing to wear," Avery says, followed by a deep sigh.

Looking from one side of her to the other, there are easily thirty pieces of clothing on her floor. She follows my gaze and shrugs.

"It all feels like sad clothes," she says.

Sad ... clothes? That's new to me.

"What are sad clothes?"

"Not happy clothes."

"Right. I totally understand. Let's see what we can find in here, then, and hopefully we won't need to shop for a new wardrobe before the day is over, yeah?" I say stepping into the closet with her and picking up pants and shirts to lay on her bed. "What are happy colors?"

"All the rainbow colors."

Simple enough. I can handle the rainbow.

"You wanted jeans, right?" Standing beside me next to her bed, Avery nods. Picking up a pair of teal jeans, I say, "Here, what about these?"

She grabs them from my hand. "Those are happy pants."

Rifling through the pile of shirts I put on the bed, I find a pink T-shirt and a purple button-down sweater and hold them up. Grabbing those from my hands as well, her face splits into a smile.

"Perfect!"

As I start putting her clothes back on hangers and placing them on the bar in her closet, Avery takes her time figuring out getting her pajamas off and underwear on. When I turn around, she's sitting on the floor and got her shirt on backwards with both legs stuck in one pantleg.

"You're doing a great job. Would you like some help?" I ask, trying to keep myself from laughing.

Avery doesn't even answer me, just looks up at me with sad eyes. I kneel in front of her and wiggle the jeans from her legs, holding the waist open so she can stick both legs in their respective holes and then push them up her calves to free her feet. Pulling her to standing, she pulls them up the rest of the way, buttoning and zipping before I help her with her shirt. In the quiet, I hold her sweater open and she pushes one arm in its sleeve, then the other, and turns in a circle to show off her outfit.

"It's amazing. I love it. Very you," I say, admiring her bold style. "I hope you never change and always wear happy clothes. Now, should we brush your hair or are we going for the bedhead look?"

"Are you going to marry my mom? So, you can be my dad?" she asks, seemingly out of nowhere. But I know it's not from nowhere. I know this kid has good hearing and she's not immune to the little conversations here and there.

Taking a moment before responding, I sit on the edge of her bed and, resting my elbows on my knees, I clasp my hands together. I need a second to think because this isn't a conversation I should be having alone with a preschooler, but Avery isn't an average preschooler. She's never been average.

"I think marrying your mom and being your dad would be the best thing ever. But it's up to Mom whether she wants that for us," I say, choosing my words carefully.

"But you want to marry us? Right?" she asks, reaching out to hold my hands in hers. "You love us?"

"With every fiber of my being."

"Good." She pulls my hands apart and pushes into my bubble to hug me. "Thank you for being my dad."

Holding her snuggly to me, I kiss her head, breathe in the scent of her kid's shampoo, and try to keep the tears at bay.

"Thank you for letting me," I choke out, tightening my grip.

Throughout this entire journey — playing the uncle to Avery because her mom and I were good friends, to the surrogacy with Elise, to loving Elise and Avery as fully and completely as I can without them legally being my family — this is a moment I wasn't prepared for. I was hardly prepared for my sister to tell Elise to just hurry up and marry me, but for Avery to want that for us is a bigger step. It feels bigger because it is bigger. It's massive. Why? Because she has a father and she cares about him despite him not showing his love for her in the ways she needs it. I know I won't replace Tanner, but I'll be damned if I'm not going to try to outdo him in every way to make sure Avery knows how much she's wanted and needed.

When she pulls away from me and goes running from the room, I can't make myself move. Instead, I sit in a bedroom that I designed for a child before there was ever a child for the bedroom. There are two other rooms identical to this, and one is slowly being filled with diapers and clothes and a rocking chair that matches the one I bought for Avery's room when Elise was pregnant with her. I've spent the last decade trying to create a reality for myself that really wasn't meant to come true because it was just me.

Alone. For so long, it was just me. Deep down, I was afraid it would always be just me. But in the span of a year, I have gone from wishing and hoping I would have a family and keeping my bigger plans a secret from everyone, to the rooms in my home being filled with toys and laughter and love.

She clears her throat at the doorway and when I look up, she's leaning against the frame studying me.

"She wants me to be her dad," I say.

"I know," she says. "I've known for a while."

"Do you?" I ask. I wait. I hope that she feels the same way I do, that Avery does. When the conversation about Avery being my daughter came up the other night, she didn't comment on how I feel about it. She just let it be, but I need to know. "Do you want me to be her dad?"

Her expression doesn't change as she watches me watching her.

"I can't want what I already have, Damian."

Pushing away from the doorframe, Elise walks over and comes to a stop, her feet in line between mine. Her maternity shirt is pulled snug around her midsection, and as I wrap my hands around the backs of her thighs to pull her closer to me, I kiss the top of her bump.

"With everything that has been said and has happened in the last twenty-four hours, all the truths and honesty, I don't want anyone else to be her dad. She has a father. That's the role he's always been in. You've always stepped up for me and for her. Even when I was just your sister's annoying little friend."

"You were never annoying," I say.

"Lies. I was annoying. All preteen girls are. My point is, even if Tanner wasn't a complete waste of space, you would still be a bonus parent. You just aren't a bonus anymore. You're a parent. You're her parent. She sees you as her dad, and that's the most important job you're ever going to have. End of discussion."

Laying my cheek on her belly, she gently strokes my hair. Despite everything we've been through, I didn't see Elise comforting me as an option. I've always wanted to be the guy who comforts her, but our experiences over the last several months — all the conversations about feelings and roles in this relationship — have taught me one thing. We want to both be authentic, and part of my authenticity is being an emotional guy.

"I'm scared," I say, quietly. With my eyes closed, I draw in a ragged breath. Of all the things I've admitted to her, this isn't one of them. I've been excited and nervous, but to tell her I'm scared hasn't happened. "I'm scared I'll mess it up."

"Mess what up?" she asks, never letting her hand stop moving as she brushes her fingers along my scalp.

"Being a parent. Being Avery's dad. Us," I say. "What if I'm not enough for all of you?"

"That's a lie you need to not tell yourself. How many times have you reminded me to not think like that?"

"A lot."

"And that's because those thoughts are lies. You can be scared, Damian. We're all scared we're going to screw up parenting. My parents, your parents, me, the lady at the grocery store ... and, honestly, we're going to screw up. Don't be surprised when you have to apologize to the kids for being wrong or for being unintentionally mean because you had a hard day and got triggered by something they do," she says. The words are hard and honest, but she says them softly, speaking to my heart and my brain at the same time. "Being scared is a normal response to parenthood. This isn't supposed to be easy. But we're in it together. In a way, we always have been."

Sliding my arms up over her bottom and wrapping them tighter around her waist, I breathe her in deeply and nestle my cheek into the softness of her firm belly.

"What was that?" I ask, my eyes popping open.

"That would be your baby kicking you in the face," she says, laughing. "You're squishing him. Or her."

I've felt the slight rolling when the baby moves, but anytime Elise has tried to get me to feel more than that the baby stops.

"Is it always that hard?" I ask, looking up at her.

She twists my hair in her fingers and then takes my face in her hands, her features softening.

"Not always, but they're trying to stretch those little legs. Too bad for them, we've still got a few months to go and it's only going to get more cramped in there."

Placing my lips against her shirt, I kiss where those little feet were a moment ago.

"I love you," I whisper to her belly. Looking up at Elise again, I say, "I love you."

"I love you, too," she says, pulling me up from the bed. I lean in and kiss her mouth, gently taking everything she's willing to give. Breaking away from me with a smile she asks, "Now, can we go get ready to eat cake?"

*****

"I like the vanilla bean cake with raspberry filling. This buttercream is to die for," Julia says, licking the back of her fork. "Can I just order a bucket of the frosting? Do you think she would allow that?"

"But the chocolate. It tastes like a brownie but it's fluffy and moist and … how?" Angela says, turning her fork in hand and inspecting the bite of cake before popping it in her mouth.

I didn't want to encroach on the girl time thing Angela and Elise had planned, but they both wanted my opinion as well. Julia has fit right into the fold since she walked through the door and I'm so glad my sister was willing to meet her "not replacement," which was the only way she would refer to Jullia until she met her.

Watching each of them react to the cakes Ang brought home to try has been nothing short of comical as they scrutinize each piece.

"I like them all. Mommy, can we just get all of them?" Avery asks.

"Where is this place again?" Elise asks my sister. "Maybe I should stop trying to make homemade cakes for birthdays and just order from her."

Putting Angela in charge of the cake was the best idea. She knows her sweets, and likes quality food, so I knew she'd bring her A game. I just didn't expect her to find a bakery that's two hundred miles away and not even bother looking closer to home.

"They're in Brockport. It's called The Bakery on Main and it's such a sweet little shop. She's got a food truck, too. It's crazy. I can't wait to get food from there regularly," she says, then stops and looks at me with a shocked expression on her face. "I mean, because I come home so often. I can stop there regularly."

Elise and Julia didn't miss it either. All three of us stare at Angela.

"Truth or dare?" Elise says to Angela.

"Dare."

"I dare you to tell me how regularly you plan to visit this bakery."

"That's not a fair dare," Angela says.

"It's totally fair," I say. "Out with it."

Getting up from the table to refill her glass of milk, Angela takes her time to answer us. We wait patiently. Most of us do, anyway.

"Aunt Ang, we're not getting any younger here."

Hiding my smile behind my hand, I look at my sister. Hopefully it's an encouraging look because I don't want her to feel like we're going to be disappointed by what she's going to tell us.

"Mac said he wouldn't hire me on if I moved back home. I took your advice to explore the in between areas. Turns out, Brockport is like home, but not home, and I sort of fell in love with it," she says. "There are colleges nearby and I took a chance at sending my resume to a few of them."

"And?" Elise asks, sitting at the edge of her seat as my sister stands beside me at the counter. I can see the excitement growing in her eyes at the possibility of my sister moving closer to home again.

"And starting in March I'll be in Brockport full time. I found an apartment near campus so I can walk to work when the weather is nice. It's the kind of college town I wish I had lived in when I was in school," she says as Elise and Avery jump up and smother her in hugs. "I just ... I really hated Buffalo. There's nothing wrong with Buffalo, I just don't want to be split between two big campuses and in offices with people who have worked with me for months and still don't take the time to know my name. I miss my small town."

Stepping into their hug huddle, I wrap my arm around my sister's shoulder and pull all three of them to me. Then, noticing Julia sitting at the dining room table watching the entire scene like a lonely puppy, I motion her over.

"Come on. You're part of this happy announcement, too," I say.

It takes her a beat to get up from her seat and come over to join us.

"This is really exciting, Angela," she says.

"Right? This means the three of us can spend more time together," Angela says smiling at Julia. "I can't wait to hang out more. This one time is not nearly enough."

Elise looks up at me, grinning because she's accomplished what she thought might be an impossible task, and that was getting her best friend to be open to the idea of more connections.

When the hugs end, Avery runs back to finish the piece of cake she was tasting before going to play while I clean up the mess. The big girls start talking about the best flavors and what should go on the cake, but before the conversation gets too in depth, Angela grabs her empty glass to bring to the sink.

"I'm proud of you," I say, leaning in so only she hears me. Reiterating something Elise said this morning, I say, "I know none of this was easy."

She shrugs, and looks up at me with a half-smile.

"It really wasn't. Moving last year was hard, admitting defeat was harder. I'm glad I listened when all of you told me to get off the beaten path. Easier said than done, but I'm figuring out that things aren't always meant to be easy. We don't learn to grow by standing still."

"Guess we're both learning lessons we didn't plan to," I say.

She gives me a questioning look and I feel the need to elaborate, even if only slightly.

"I had my own little freak out earlier about being scared that I won't be a good dad or enough for them. It was nothing."

"That's not nothing," she says. "I'm glad you can admit you're worried about things like that. Not a lot of guys would. ... I'm proud of you, too, you know?"

Leaning into Angela's shoulder, I put our heads together and we watch Julia and Elise work out a list of their favorite parts about the cakes they tasted. The markers have made an appearance so they can color code everything and I almost suggest they pull out the poster board, but stop short and laugh at myself for the thought.

"I know you are," I say. "We've come a long way, kid."

Chapter 23

ELISE

Somehow the last eight weeks have flown by and I've been too exhausted to notice. With the exception of Angela moving from Buffalo to Brockport, and me and Damian going out to help with the move, every day has been similar.

I get up in the middle of the night twice to pee. I wake up after hitting snooze three times, take a shower, Damian gets Avery up while I try to put socks on, he comes in and helps me with my socks, then makes me sit at the table while he makes us breakfast.

"I could do that," I say as he starts the stove on Thursday morning. "I'm not incapable."

"No, you're not. I would never say that," he says, cracking eggs into a dish to whisk them for omelets. "But I will say, that little person in there is making it more difficult for you to use the stove safely. Plus, just let me do this for you. I enjoy it."

Leaning on the table I watch him as he moves around the kitchen and I fully believe he enjoys cooking for us. It's one thing we have always bonded over, but this isn't about bonding. This is about me not setting my shirt on fire. Again.

"When is Angela going to be home for the shower?" I ask, rubbing my belly as I stand up to get out plates. I call into the living room, "Aves, time to pick up. Breakfast is almost ready."

"She said she'd be here tomorrow before dinner so she can decorate a little with you because, and these are her words, she doesn't want you overdoing it and going into labor early," he says, using the spatula as a microphone. "I think she's going to jinx things talking like that, but if things haven't been jinxed yet I don't see it happening now."

He started looking up Old Wives' Tales about pregnancy a couple weeks ago, then panicked when I got my hair cut — it was just a trim, so nothing crazy — because there's an old superstition about the baby being bald or having bad vision if the mother gets her hair cut while pregnant. Don't even get me started on how he reacted to me reaching above my head. Just because I reach up into a high cupboard to get something down does not, under any circumstances, mean the umbilical cord is going to wrap around the baby's neck. I told him to stay off the internet because he was driving me crazy.

"I wish you would focus on the fun tales, like about heartrate and how I'm carrying," I say.

"It's twins. I'm convinced one of them is hiding. Also, the internet says you're carrying like it's a boy, so now we just wait to see who's right," he says, pointing at me with his spatula. "Angela thinks it's a girl."

"Shut your whore mouth, Damian. It is not twins," I say, laughing until tears form. "You've been to every ultrasound. There's only one. There's only ever been one. If you keep this up, you'll manifest twins for the next pregnancy and I don't know if there's enough room in there for two considering how big this one is."

Placing an omelet for Avery on her plate, he leans in and kisses my cheek.

"I think you would be adorable with twins."

"Definitely adorable," I say. "And more exhausted."

He shrugs. I shrug.

"Twins wouldn't be horrible ..." I say, but walk away to check on Avery before he can respond.

The more this child grows the more I waddle. It's like they're sitting in my lap already and I could still have eight or more weeks. My lower back hurts. My pelvis is sore. My skin is dry and itchy. I know it's way too early to be thinking about meeting this person, but they could maybe do me a favor and quit jabbing me right in the cervix.

A sharp intake of breath and I stop in my tracks.

"That hurts, dude," I say, cradling my abdomen as I wait for the sensation to pass. "You need to stop that or your Aunt Ang isn't going to let me help with anything tomorrow."

"Mommy, are you okay?" Avery asks as she comes to stand beside me. "Is my baby being mean?"

We've had this conversation before about how the baby kicks and rolls and stretches, and it's not always comfortable for me. She's slowly put together that sometimes it hurts, so naturally in her mind it's because the baby is being mean.

"Not mean, Sunshine, just stretching. Are you ready for breakfast? Damian made omelets."

As she runs back to the kitchen, I hobble to the recliner and sit down. We definitely did not take Damian's height into full account when we agreed to this baby. It feels like there's a head in my crotch and a butt in my ribs.

"How am I supposed to do this for eight more weeks?"

"Carefully," he says, coming up behind the chair. Reaching over the back of the recliner, he gently begins pressing his thumbs into my shoulders and working the knots out of my muscles. "Maybe you should call into work today. Take a sick day."

"I can't. I'm already taking tomorrow off. I don't want to leave Julia hanging two days in a row," I say, dropping my head back to look up at him.

"Then at least try to sit as much as you can," he says, a worried expression marring his beautiful face. "I know there's supposed to be plenty of time, but I don't want you overdoing it."

"I won't. You've put Julia on watchdog duty so aside from the teaching aspect, she's not letting me do a whole lot of extra," I say. "Did I tell you she scolded me yesterday for standing too long and then when I did sit down, she made me put my feet up on one of the extra classroom chairs."

He laughs, and unsuccessfully hides it behind his hand.

"Yeah, you told me. I didn't mean for her to go that extreme. Let's be realistic, though. If she didn't remind you to sit occasionally or to drink your water or any of that stuff, would you do it?"

I roll my eyes at him and look back down at my swollen belly. Reaching behind me, I grab his hand and pull it over me to lay his hand on the bump.

"Why is it so hard?" he asks, concerned.

"Braxton Hicks. It's just practice, but it's been happening more this week."

"It feels so weird," he says, his eyebrows drawn together as he studies my body beneath his hand.

"Just wait until the real deal and they're one on top of another and I'm telling you how much I think you suck. That's always a fun time," I say, amused at his reaction.

"I might suck, but you love us enough to be thinking about another one after this, so ..."

Bringing his other hand around to envelop me, he places them both on my belly and I lay mine on top of his.

"Are you planning on an epidural?" he asks.

We haven't talked about that part, but I didn't have one with Avery and haven't put much thought into having one this time around.

"I'd rather not, but if it comes down to it and I need to rest, I might ask for one. I don't want to say absolutely not and then absolutely yes want one, you know? It's possible this baby will come just as quickly as Avery and I won't have time for one. Or I just might want you to see me suffer to the full extent," I say, tipping my forehead against the side of his head. "You know, just to keep things in our relationship exciting."

"You're horrible lately," he says, laughing. "But I think you know your body well enough to know if and when you want to numb the pain. Something tells me I'm not going to deal well with you hurting."

I snort out a laugh. This is a guy who got visibly upset when I stubbed my toe last week. He's going to need anesthesia, not me.

"You'll be okay," I lie. "All right, help me up. I need to eat and leave. Avery's bus is going to be here soon."

Damian walks around to face me, reaching out to grab my hands and pull me up from the chair.

"I really cannot wait until I can get out of furniture on my own again."

"Soon," he says, leaning in to kiss me. "Soon."

*****

All day at work, Braxton Hicks. I drank water. I sat. I almost called my doctor. Julia told Laura after lunch, and Laura took over my class and sent me home early.

Damian is in his office when I come through the door. Avery is in with him, at her own kid sized drafting table, and barely notices when I poke my head in. She must be working on a big project. She's been hell bent to help him since the indoor playground concept. I don't keep it a secret that I love watching them work on things together.

"You're home early," he says, looking up from his computer. Then he glances at the clock on his desk. "Really early. What's wrong?"

"Nothing. Much. Nothing much. Just a lot of tightening, baby hiccups, and I feel like my pelvis is breaking. So, yeah, nothing major. Just growing a human," I say, trying to downplay the entire pregnancy thing.

"Hospital?"

166

"It's not that bad. I'm going to get some water and lay down. I love you," I say, knowing if I don't actually go lay down, he's going to pick me up and carry me to the nearest soft surface to rest.

I waddle away and as soon as I'm comfortable on the couch, I send a message to Angela.

Me: Can't wait for you to be home. I can use all the help I can get.

Setting the phone down on top of my bump, I grab the book I've been trying to read. Trying. Every night I fall asleep a page into reading and then wake up having to find my spot all over again. At this point, I don't even know what this is about and should just start over or listen to the audiobook.

My phone buzzes with an incoming message from Ang and as I move the offending device, a tiny baby butt pushes up to the top of my abdomen.

"No naughtiness, little one," I say, poking the hard spot on my belly.

I'll never get used to the feeling of someone moving around in there. However, if it's anything like after Avery was born, I'm going to miss it almost as soon as they're born.

Ang: Damian just messaged me and said they sent you home early. Is someone causing you issues? They realize there are still six weeks of growing left, right?

Smiling at her message, I remember how adamant she was that Avery couldn't come early. Unfortunately, Aves was a show off and came two weeks early, much to Angela's disappointment. My due date was her birthday and she was hoping for a birthday twin. Silly? Yes. But she warmed up to it once she realized we get to eat cake twice in one month.

Me: Aunt Ang might have to come have a chat with them about that.

It's maybe ten seconds after I send the message that she calls me.

"It's not bad. It's just reminiscent of Avery's last few weeks on the inside. That's all."

"Right, which is what concerns me. You need to tell Mac you're done until after the baby comes. Or, how about this ... just be done with the diner?"

She's brought this up before, but I love my nights at the diner.

"This didn't even start on a diner night, Angela," I say, defensively.

She sighs. I sigh.

"Plus, this baby is measuring bigger than Avery did at this age. Damian is tall, the egg donor is tall, this kid is all legs and has a head full of hair already," I say, giggling. "All things Avery wasn't. I mean, Tanner is barely an inch taller than me and she got my normal length legs."

"Yeah, Tanner is pretty tiny for a dude," she says. "Speaking of, have you heard anything?"

That's a loaded question. I've heard lots — like how I'm a selfish bitch for letting their son sit in a jail cell in Austin and that none of them want anything to do with me or Avery because of my "lack of empathy."

"You don't want to know all the things his family has said to me, but he's still hanging out in his eight-by-eight cement bedroom thinking about his actions and how sometimes, they really do have consequences," I say.

She hardly contains her laughter.

"I love you so much."

"I know, right? I'm pretty amazing. I love you, too." There's a moment of quiet and I hear her typing on her computer. But it's more than that. I hear how relaxed she is. "I also love how awesome this new job is for you. You sound so much happier."

"I really am. The transition has been seamless and I feel like I belong here. Like, this is home. It feels like home. It's weird. Plus, everyone here seems ... genuine," she says. "Which reminds me. Delilah called earlier and said the cakes are done. I can pick up in the morning before heading back to Cooperstown so I don't have to figure out how to store them in my little fridge. I might grab scones from the coffeeshop, too. Or cinnamon rolls."

At the mention of baked goods, my mouth begins watering.

"Please stop talking. All of that sounds so good and I can't even eat it until tomorrow afternoon at the earliest," I say.

"Fine. I'll stop. It'll be worth the wait though, promise."

We chat a few more minutes until a wave of exhaustion hits me and I can't contain the yawning anymore.

"You sleep, and I'll see you tomorrow. Tell that baby to quit it or we're having a chat when I get home," she says, her tone lighthearted and nothing but love for her niece or nephew.

"Sounds good. Drive safe. I'll see you soon. Love you."

"Love you, too."

*****

The living room is dark when I open my eyes. The only light visible is the moon as it shines in through the floor-to-ceiling windows overlooking the lake and it takes my breath away. When Avery and I were living in an apartment across town, I didn't think much about what I was missing by not having a house. But this? I was missing this. It's serene and a much better view than the parking lot I shared with all our neighbors.

I stretch and make a concerted effort to get off the couch, rolling off and sitting on the floor on my knees to start the process, and notice a dim light in the kitchen is still on. Glancing at my watch, it's after Avery's bedtime, and a touch of sadness presses into my chest at not kissing her goodnight.

Damian is sitting at the table in just a pair of sweatpants when I wander in to turn the light off and, before he can notice me, I take a long look at him. When we were younger, he was just a scrawny boy, bony shoulders and every ounce the nerd that he still is. But now, that boy is just a faded memory as I take in the breadth of his back, the muscles he's built from years of working out, hard work on different projects, and more recently while also building the indoor playground downstairs. Walking up behind him, I trail my fingers along the tops of his shoulders, following them with kisses on his bare back.

"I thought I heard you," he says, gruffly, never stopping his hand from moving as he sketches a new project. "I tried waking you for dinner, but you were out cold."

Reaching up with his free hand, he captures my fingers and pulls them around to his lips, gently kissing the tips.

"Who doesn't need a five-hour nap once in a while?" I say. "I'm still tired, though."

Sitting up straight, Damian shifts in his seat and simultaneously leads me around to sit on his lap. I barely fit between him and the table, but we make it work as I lay my head on his shoulder while he cradles me in his arms.

"I'm just finishing up and then I'll be in. You want anything to eat before going to bed?"

"Applesauce and a grilled cheese," I say.

He chuckles as he strokes my back, but neither of us move.

"Do you think we'll be ready if the baby comes early?" I ask. It's been a topic we've discussed, but only in passing, and mostly as a joke. With the way I was feeling all day, I don't think we should tease about it anymore. "Aves was early and she was smaller."

"Those measurements could be wrong."

"I know, but he feels bigger, too. I can't describe it. Do you think we'll be ready?" I ask again.

I'm not sure if he thinks I mean "ready" in the sense we'll have the rest of the nursery set up and clothes washed. I mean ready to be parents together. I've worked through my concerns about parenting this little one, and I know Damian is a great dad — I see it every day with Avery — but it's different coming into parenting when you're already done with the infant stage. Yes, he was around and helping me when Avery was a baby, but not all the time. This time, he's starting from scratch. He's going to suffer through the sleep regressions and the growth spurts and the crying we can't figure out from the very beginning.

"I think we're going to be as ready as we can be, Elise. Even with a five-year-old, we still aren't ready some days. We certainly aren't winging it, but we aren't starting from nothing, either," he says. "I want you to worry about getting to the finish line. Worry about opening gifts with me and Avery on Saturday. Worry about having a snack and going back to bed. Those are things we can control right now."

Nodding my head, I slide off his lap and go to the stove. I don't even want a whole grilled sandwich, just half. Maybe with a pickle in the middle. Gathering my supplies and starting the stove, I pop the top off one of Avery's applesauce pouches and start sucking it down.

"What are you doing?" Damian says from across the room.

"Making food like you told me to."

I fish a sandwich slice pickle from the jar and bite it. Buttering the bread for my sandwich, I move to place the first piece in the pan and stop to stare at the stove.

"Were you planning to use a dish?"

Closing my eyes, I take a steadying breath.

"I was getting to that part."

"Yup," he says, pushing up from his chair. He walks with an exaggerated swagger, showing his confidence in each step as he makes his way closer to me. Opening the cupboard and sliding a pan from within, he never takes his eyes off me. He winks as he places the skillet on the burner. "I got you."

"How do you keep getting hotter?" I ask him, forgetting my filter but knowing I don't need it with him.

"I've just paid attention to the things you need and want. I respond accordingly. It's not that hard. You do it, too," he says, kissing my cheek. Unsure of myself or how to respond, I feel my forehead wrinkle as I look at him. "What? You have that 'he's full of shit but I don't know how to say it' expression on your face."

Scrunching my lips together, I bite the inside of my cheek.

"You know not every man is like that, right? I've known you forever and it still feels foreign to me sometimes that you see a thing happening and adjust. You fix the behavior or explain the situation and you don't yell at me or tell me I'm wrong," I say. "I was about to toss a slice of buttered bread on the stovetop without a pan and you just ... got up to get me a pan. It's so normal for you to do things like that and I just need you to know how much I appreciate everything you have given me. Ever. You've loved me forever and I sometimes wonder why I couldn't show you I loved you back before things got messy."

His eyes soften and I realize this is a conversation we've had many times, almost too many, but I need him to know he's not typical. That's one of the things I love most about him.

"It had to be messy in order for us to find one another, Elise. I will take all the messy years of standing behind you, of catching you when you've fallen, for a future filled with standing beside you," he says. "It's not that things aren't messy now. They're just different messy. I still mess up. You do, too. But we learn from those mistakes and we only grow stronger together because of it."

"I'm really lucky to have you. I don't know if you know how many times you've saved me, and I know you've said Avery and I are the reason you've stayed here, but you're the reason I never gave up on the idea of finding real love. You showed me every single day that it was possible to love me even when I felt the least lovable, and I can't ever thank you enough for that," I say, sniffing back tears I didn't intend to shed tonight.

When he brushes his thumbs along my cheeks and cradles my face in his hands, the tears begin running down my face and I can't stop them.

"I love you harder on the days you feel the worst because those are the days you need it most. When you're down, I lift you up. When you're afraid, I'll be here to protect you," he says, leaning in to kiss away the tears. "When you're filled with joy, I will be celebrating right beside you."

M.L. PENNOCK

Chapter 24

DAMIAN

"Where do you want me to put these wipes?" Julia asks, holding up an economy size box of baby wipes.

"Bottom dresser drawer," Elise says, then stops herself. With her pointer finger stuck to the tip of her nose as she completes her thought, she says, "Actually, do you mind taking all the packs out of the box and then putting them in the drawer?"

Julia laughs as she walks down the hall, calling back over her shoulder, "I was already planning to."

Turning to me and Angela, Elise mouths "I kinda love her" to us.

"What about the burp cloths?" Angela asks, laughing as she stands up from her spot on the living room floor.

"Laundry basket. All the cloth things need to be washed," Elise says, and I audibly question what she means by cloth things. "The burp rags, the newborn size clothes, the little socks, and a few hats. It's still going to be chilly in May. Or April. As long as it's not before April."

She's still concerned about going into labor really early, but my mom, her mom, and every other woman in our house today who has been pregnant or been around pregnant people told her she hasn't dropped yet. Since I know she's stressing out, I tried to be funny and asked what she's supposed to drop ... and the looks I got almost burned a hole in my face. Thankfully, they all eased up slightly and realized I was attempting comical relief, but not before my life flashed before my eyes. Plus, the refresher on what the phrase means was helpful since I don't remember that happening when she was pregnant with Avery.

"I can work on getting the rest of the clothes sorted and hang up the things we won't need right away if you ladies want to put your feet up and rest," I offer.

"Are you sure?" Elise asks, opening a pack of miniature T-shirts and tossing them in with the laundry that needs to be washed. "There's still so much to do."

Angela and I share a look, and a moment later she picks up the other basket filled with clothes needing to be sorted and hung, then leaves the room.

"I've got a handle on it, Leesy," I say, coming up on my knees and crawling over to her. Placing my hands on her legs and sliding them up her thighs, I push her feet apart and slip into the V that has formed. "You don't have to do it all."

Kissing her belly, I remind her that she should be relaxing right now. Soon enough she's going to have the urge to clean everything. That nesting instinct is going to kick in and then I won't be able to keep her from cleaning and rearranging the entire house. That part I do remember from the end of her pregnancy with Aves. She was practically manic and only had a small apartment. I can only imagine how stressful it's going to get with a big house.

Her fingers trace circles in my hair, fluffing it up, and I relax against her abdomen with my ear planted against the top of her belly.

"Do you think the baby is going to have your hair or hers?"

"I don't know. I like to think my genes are strong, but we both know genetics are wild," I say.

This is the first time she's voiced concern about who the baby is going to look like and I don't want that to become an issue, but at the same time I need to know what she's thinking.

"Are you afraid they're going to look more like her than like me?" I ask, building myself up for the next question that's suddenly weighing on me.

"I think they're going to look like you as a newborn and grow into her features later on. It feels like that's how it was with Avery. She looked so much like Tanner when she was fresh out of the oven, but now she's my mini me."

"Are you afraid you'll love them less if they look like her?"

I hear her breath hitch, but can't lift my eyes to look at her. Her fingers stop moving in my hair and it's like I hit the pause button on our entire future. What if she's unsure? What if she thinks she won't have room to love them fully if they don't have my eyes, my nose? How would we move beyond that?

"My love doesn't come with conditions. This child could look like the woman who delivers the mail and I will still love them with every fiber of my soul, Damian."

I release a sigh of relief, feeling silly for doubting her feelings. Her fingers begin massaging my scalp once more, putting my entire body at ease. Like a wave coming ashore, there's movement inside her belly and Elise sits up a little taller in her seat prompting me to lift my head to look at her.

"Baby gymnastics tonight, huh?"

"Or making a final attempt to be head down. I'm pretty sure that's a butt," she says, poking a small protrusion on her left side. Then sliding her hand down toward her lap she says, "Which means, there's a head right about there."

"This kid is going to be huge if you make it to your due date," I say without taking a second to think first.

She laughs and takes my face into her hands, pulling me up from the floor so she can reach my mouth. Kissing my lips once, twice, three times, she lets me go and puts her hands out for me to take.

"That's what I've been saying," she says, as I lift her from the chair. "We're not going to get anywhere near that due date at the rate we're going. It doesn't help that I want to start deep cleaning the baseboards."

"No. Not yet. It's too soon. No baseboards," I say.

"Fine. No baseboards until at least April. Is that better."

"Much."

*****

Julia headed for home close to dinner time so Angela, Elise, and Avery decided to have snacks instead of a real meal. Plus, there's plenty of cake left to nibble on. I'm sure we could also freeze some to eat when the baby is born. A little extra celebration motivation to get through those first several nights at home with a newborn, you know?

"So ... do you think you'll make it home in time when I go into labor?" Elise asks, seemingly out of the blue. For those of us who know her as well as we do, we're aware this is something that has likely weighed heavily on her mind. "I mean, you were here when I had Avery and are a huge part of my support system. My mom has been great, I just ... never mind."

Angela and I look at each other from opposite sides of the dining room table. It's a knowing look.

"I will do my absolute best to get here in time. The weather is on our side unless there's a freak snowstorm. Plus, if this kid plans it right, school with be in recess," she says.

Elise raises an eyebrow. We all know what college schedules look like, and spring break is this coming week, which means we are still six weeks from our due date.

"No. There is absolutely no way this kid is going to stay in until after the semester ends," Elise says, horrified Angela would suggest such a thing. "You'll be lucky if I make it to May at all."

I watch as my sister breaks down in laughter, enjoying the moment, before catching her breath and saying, "I know. I don't expect him to wait. That child is already huge, I'll be surprised if you make it to the middle of April."

Popping a piece of cheese in her mouth, Angela takes her time chewing.

"I'll be here. No worries. Someone just needs to call me as soon as those contractions are consistent and I'll be on the road," she says.

The energy in the room shifts and there's a calmness that surrounds us.

"Am I staying with you while Mommy is at the hospital?" Avery asks, the question pointed in Angela's direction.

"Absolutely. If the baby is born in the middle of the night, though, and Mom wants me to stay with her and Damian, maybe Grandma can come hang with you," Angela says.

Elise and I have already discussed those plans and figured one mom or the other would be here with Avery. I guess if Aves wants Angela to stay with her while we wait to be discharged from the hospital, we'll roll with it.

"No matter what, though, someone will be with you. You don't have to stress about that, Sunshine," Angela says, then with a pointed glance in my direction, she adds, "No one needs to stress about anything. It'll all work out."

Chapter 25

ELISE

"You shouldn't be here, young lady."

There's no point in arguing with him. I told Mac I would stop working a week ago, but here I am, refilling sugar jars and napkin holders.

"At least I'm sitting down," I say, wiggling a bit on the stool to get more comfortable. It's hard to be comfy when you have a basketball in your lap all day, every day. "If I hadn't come here, I would be at home trying to not clean things since Damian told me I'm not allowed to start nesting yet. He's worried I'll overdo it."

Spinning on the stool, I face Mac and give him a sly grin.

"But what he doesn't notice won't hurt him."

"I'm calling him."

"You can't! Mac, that's not fair. It was just some light dusting and mopping. Maybe a little reorganizing the utility closet."

"I don't need you going into labor here again, Elise. Once was enough."

"I swear, I'm not going to go into labor here. I just needed to get away for a little bit," I say, enjoying the quiet of the diner before busy hours. "I'm almost thirty-six weeks pregnant and just wanted to come hang out. I promise not to take anyone's orders or bus any tables while I'm here visiting."

He gives me an unconvinced look, but goes about his business behind the counter.

"How's Angela doing with the new place?"

"Really great. She loves the job, the town, the people, everything. Plus, she's closer to home without being home, which was the goal, remember?"

Lifting a mug of steaming coffee to his lips, he nods. She was home the entire week she had off for spring break and it was glorious. It didn't line up with my break at work or Avery's spring break since they follow the same schedule with a mid-winter break in February and then another in April, but we still spent as many hours together as we could. We washed and folded a majority of the baby's new clothes that we'll need right away and between the four of us, meal prepped enough food to get me and Damian through the first week of having a new baby in the house. I've missed doing normal things like that with my best friend. I do them all the time with her brother, but I've definitely missed doing the mundane with Angela.

"Yup. So, what's wrong?"

"Nothing. Much," I say.

When I look at him again, his fatherly eyes are boring a hole into me. They're like a truth serum – he always gets my honesty. Plus, I can't be bothered lying to him. He's one of my most trusted adults and I respect him for taking the time to care enough to listen.

"Just worried she won't make it in time when I do go into labor. It's still a long drive, even if it is closer. She swears she'll be here, but what if she isn't?"

Leaning his elbows on the counter, Mac clasps his hands around his mug and stares into the liquid as if it has the answers for my issue. When he starts stroking his greying beard, I know he's thinking hard.

"Penny for your thoughts?"

"I think it's really admirable that you not only are having this baby for Damian, but you're also worried about your best friend making it home in time to be there with you both," he says. I hear a 'but' coming, though, and sit tight waiting for him to continue. "Just, make sure you're thinking about you, too."

Nodding, I finish filling the last napkin holder and set it in a row with the others.

"This is why I needed to come visit today. Sometimes, I forget to think about myself. It's difficult to, especially when I've spent so many years thinking about Avery before anyone else, including me."

"But that's what mothers do. You put everyone above you. You can't pour from an empty cup, though, and that's the part you really need to remember," he says. "I'm glad you decided to fill your cup here today, kid."

We continue to exist in comfortable silence for a few minutes as he focuses on busywork and I take the napkin holders back to the tables I snatched them from. There are only a few people in the diner, here primarily because it's the in-between hours — lunch is long over but dinner is still a while away — so they can enjoy an afternoon cup of coffee without too many people bothering them. There's no one waiting for their table and they're well known enough by the small staff that, aside from refilling their coffee and tea and soda, they're largely left alone.

Stepping behind the counter to grab a carafe, there's a sharp pain that radiates from my pelvis up into my abdomen. It's painful enough that I draw in a tense breath loudly and, unfortunately, it catches Mac's attention.

"Elise?"

"I'm good. Just growing pains," I say, and keep moving.

I walk slowly from one table to another, arranging condiments and topping off mugs with fresh coffee when I come up to one of my regular couples.

"Oh my, Elise, I thought you were done here for a while?" Edna says.

"I am. I'm not working today."

"But ..." she points to the carafe in my hand while giving a knowing smile to her husband across from her.

"Avery is home with Damian and I got bored. Needed to do something other than sit in the house," I say, smiling.

"I remember those days. Just take it easy, okay?"

"Yes, ma'am. I'm heading back home in a few minutes, anyway. I've been here for an hour or two and get the feeling Mac is ready to kick me out since I won't just sit and do paperwork instead of visiting with all of you. Have a wonderful night," I say, smiling.

I turn to walk away and another pain comes.

As I set the carafe back on the warmer, Mac appears in the doorway between the front counter and the kitchen.

"That was, what? Maybe fifteen minutes?" he says, his eyes dropping to my belly.

"Don't, Mac. It's not contractions," I scold.

"Text me in the morning and let me know if I'm buying something purple or something green," he says, snickering. He's adamantly against pink and blue for girl and boy colors, and has been as long as I've known him, so I understand what he means as soon as he says it. "It's not contractions? Kiddo, you said that last time and we were lucky she didn't shoot out of your body right here in the dining room."

Placing my hands on my hips and attempting not to laugh, I stare at him.

"That's a bit dramatic, don't you think?"

A sobering expression comes across his face.

"No. You got to the hospital with Avery and were nine centimeters dilated. I don't think I'm being dramatic at all. I am worried, though, because

I know you still have a few weeks to go," he says. Stepping up to me, Mac places his hands on my shoulders. "Listen, if it's not contractions, great. But I still want you to go home, drink your water, watch a movie, and rest."

"Okay," I say. "I'll go rest."

"Thank you. I know it's been a long time since I was a new parent, Elise, but I still remember how exhausting it was for my wife near the end of each pregnancy," he says. "This little guy is in that final sprint to finish getting ready to meet the family. Sleep and let him grow."

My eyes well up with tears as I nod my agreement. Mac pulls me into a hug and I wrap my arms around his waist, sighing heavily.

"Go home, Elise. I don't want to see you in here again until this baby is born and you bring them to meet Uncle Mac, you hear me?"

"Loud and clear."

"Good. Now git."

*****

Curled up in the recliner with a bottle of water, a fluffy blanket, and the TV remote, I jump from one show to another. Nothing catches my interest, so when Avery comes in and wants to watch one of her movies, I agree. She snuggles up next to me with her elephant and her own blanket, and together we rest for the remainder of the afternoon.

Damian comes in with a mug of warm tea for me and leans in to kiss my forehead as he sets it on the end table beside my chair.

"You're sweaty," I say.

"You two were nice and cozy so I went for a run. I wasn't far, just laps on our road in case you needed me," he says. "How's Mac?"

Rolling my eyes slightly, I shrug.

"He was upset you were there, wasn't he?" Damian asks, smirking.

"Not upset. Just concerned. He thinks I'm going to go into labor today and now I need to prove him wrong," I say. "But I definitely dropped. This kid is so far down into my lap I had trouble sitting on the barstool. I can breathe again, though, so that's fabulous."

Damian closes his eyes, a smile crossing his lips as he shakes his head.

"Right. I'll go double check your bag for the hospital," he says.

"What? Not you, too. This baby isn't coming tonight."

"Okay," he says, and proceeds to saunter away toward the bedrooms. "Even if it isn't tonight, it's still good to have everything ready. I'll be sure to pack extra snacks for when they tell you you aren't allowed to eat."

Muttering under my breath about how no one trusts my intuition, Avery snuggles even closer to me, which I didn't think was possible. Then she encircles my belly with her arms and lays her head on it.

"The baby makes a nice pillow," she says, triggering a deep laugh from me.

"Just don't get too used to it, Sunshine. It's not going to be like that for too much longer," I say, stroking her hair as we watch the movie together. "Are you excited about the baby? We haven't talked about it too much lately, just you and me."

"Yes. I can't wait to be a big sister, Mommy," she says. Sitting up and looking at me, Avery's eyebrows wrinkle and she scrunches her nose. "I'm still a big sister even if it's not our baby, right?"

All those conversations preparing her for the fact this baby wasn't mine come back to hit me square in the chest. Damian and I have never kept the truth from her, she's known since the onset of this adventure the baby is Damain's but not mine. I just didn't take into account that we would end up where we are after all these months — fully in a relationship, cohabitating, coparenting, and loving each other as deeply as we do — and that if we didn't continue explaining things to Avery, it could hurt her in the end. Even if she does understand everything, I don't expect her to not have questions ... just like Damian asking me if I'm going to love this baby even if it has a lot of its donor's features.

I go for the simplest answer.

"Yes, you are still a big sister. Mommy and Damian plan to raise this baby together just like we're raising you together," I say.

As if she simply asked for confirmation the sky is blue, she shrugs her shoulders, smiles and says, "Okay. Just checking."

A few moments pass before she lifts her head again and looks at me.

"What's wrong?"

"So, we don't have to give the baby away?" she asks, searching for clarification.

Smiling at her, I push her hair out of her eyes and cup her face with my palm.

"No, sweetheart. We don't have to give the baby away."

She smiles and leans heavily into my hand.

"Good, because I don't think we would be able to give him away now. We love him too much."

Chapter 26

DAMIAN

She's made it another week, but not without cutting back on a lot of activity. Walking too fast, sitting for too long, standing for too long, showering, sex ... it all is either extremely uncomfortable for her, exhausts her, or causes untimeable contractions.

But, Elise's doctor just greenlit literally everything we've been cautious about.

"Did she just tell you to go have lots of sex, though?" I ask as we leave her weekly check-up. "I just want to make sure I heard her correctly."

"She kind of did. I believe she said we should try getting the baby out the same way we got it in," she says. Laughing, Elise adds, "That's going to be an awkward call to Dr. Doctor's office. I still can't get over the fact you chose the one doctor in the state whose last name is Doctor. You're such a nerd."

"Nerd, yes. But you love me regardless," he says. "Did you see her face when she realized? Priceless. I'm glad she's a good sport about it, though."

"It's not the first time I've laughed with her about being a surrogate and ending up with the baby daddy, either, or her bypassing the whole IVF thing," she says. "It's all in my chart, she's known since we started this entire thing, but has just carried on like normal the entire time. If I'm being honest, it put me at ease early on that she didn't focus on the surrogacy aspect of this pregnancy."

"I get that. I'm glad you have a doctor you fully trust. I'm sure it's not that way for everyone," I say, remembering a time when my sister switched doctors for one reason or another.

Unlocking the Yukon, I open the passenger door and hold my hand out for Elise to take as she climbs into her seat. Her body melts into the leather as she takes a second to catch her breath before buckling.

"Are you okay?" I ask cautiously. I'm sure she doesn't want me to keep asking, but I can't help it. I'm the whole reason she's in this predicament.

"Just tired," she responds, smiling without it touching her eyes. Reaching for my hand again, she looks up at me. "Let's get home. Avery will be home from school in an hour and I want to have time to relax for a little bit while you finish work."

"You got it," I say, leaning in to kiss her lips.

We set out on the thirty or so minute drive home and it's quiet. Elise has her eyes closed and is resting, her hands cradling the bottom of her belly. She thought she was carrying low last week, but now none of her shirts cover the bottom of her bump. She's started wearing my T-shirts under a button-down shirt for work because I'm tall and they cover her entire belly. It's probably a good thing next week is April break and she can just live in gym shorts and tank tops. She was planning on working until at least week thirty-nine, but that might change really soon.

Reaching across the console, I place my palm on her abdomen and feel little bumps against my hand — baby hiccups. Elise slides her hand up and covers mine. At a stoplight, I find myself staring at her left hand. Her bare fingers catch my attention and, though I know she's not a huge jewelry wearer, I wonder how she would feel about a diamond. Something small. We've talked about marriage at various times, but nothing definitive. It's all in passing and we've just gone about living life together. But I want more than—

"It's green."

"Huh?" I ask, looking up as she's caught me mid-thought.

She laughs at my expense.

"The light. It's green."

"Oh," I say, and slowly accelerate until we're up to the speed limit.

"What were you thinking about?"

"Accessories," I say, smirking but not looking at her.

*****

I wake up out of a sound sleep at 4 a.m. and she isn't in bed. I know it's silly to panic, but I panic nonetheless because these days it's rare I sleep through the night. Mostly, because she doesn't sleep through the night.

The bathroom light is on, but she isn't in there when I check. She's not in Avery's room, or the baby's room. She isn't standing in the living room where I've found her on multiple occasions as she watches the moonlight on the water.

Walking into the kitchen, I hear the unmistakable sound of a scrub brush. The counter is covered with the contents of the refrigerator. Elise stands up straight and turns to look at me, rubber gloves on and a scrubber in her hand, her hair is thrown up in a messy bun. She looks like a damn dream in a pair of my boxers and a tank top that's molded to her belly.

"Hi," she says, breathlessly. "I just ... you know, I couldn't sleep and just needed to get this done."

"I understand," I say, recalling again the end of her pregnancy with Avery when she couldn't be bothered to sit still. "I'll go through and trash the expired stuff. You don't have to do this alone."

She sighs deeply, relieved, because she still worries I'll react the way he did. I'm not him, but I don't have to tell her that. Instead, I keep doing my best to show her. I'll show her every day I'm not him if it makes life easier for her.

As she turns to wipe down a shelf in the fridge, I pull the garbage can out from beneath the sink. I go about tossing sauces and dressings that haven't been touched in months, things that should have been thrown away before Christmas.

"Are we keeping the yeast?" I ask, regarding a small jar.

"Yes. That stuff is still good. I just reused the jar." Her response comes from inside the fridge. She doesn't even take the time to look.

"What about the aloe gel? Why is there aloe in the fridge?" I ask, confused.

"Sun burns. It feels better when it's cold. It doesn't expire. I swear that shit lasts forever," she responds, looking at me over her shoulder.

When she stands up straighter to reach for the next shelf, I hear a sharp intake of breath.

"You good?" I ask. We're getting so close, but I don't want to stress her out by blatantly asking if she's having contractions.

"Yup," she says, unconvincingly. "All those things you did to me last night started something."

"If I recall correctly, you were a willing participant."

She's quiet as I begin organizing food in different categories so we can start putting things away when she's done cleaning the shelves.

"Yup," she says again, her voice tight.

"Elise?"

"I just need to finish this."

185

"How far apart are they?"

"Like, ten minutes. It could be hours before anything happens."

"Want me to call Angela?"

"Yes, please," she says. "But wait until five, then she'll be getting up anyway. She's been going to the gym before work."

I look at the clock and decide I can give my sister another half hour of sleep before starting her Friday off with a bang. Or I think I can.

"Okay, give me the milk and any other dairy stuff, except cheese," she says.

Handing her the first gallon of milk, I turn back to pick up the containers of yogurt — because doesn't everyone have six quart-size things of yogurt at all times? No? Just us? Cool — and when I attempt to hand them to Elise, she hasn't moved. She's standing in front of the fridge, holding the milk, staring at me with her mouth slightly open.

"Can you please go grab the mop and call your sister. Right now. Please," she says, and it's way too calm.

"Yes?" I say, questioning her behavior until I look down and notice a small puddle forming between her feet. "Oh, shit."

"Yeah, go."

She twists at the waist, places the milk in the fridge, then opens the drawer beside her and pulls out a stack of kitchen towels as I grab my phone on the way to the utility closet we have in the laundry room. I open the door and stand there staring at the fully organized shelves questioning if she's slept at all because I swear this wasn't like this the last time I was in here.

"When did you do that?" I ask, pushing the mop around her feet as she tries to shove a towel in her shorts to keep from leaking more amniotic fluid on the kitchen floor.

"Last week. Don't complain. It's so much better and I needed to do something to stay busy and it was driving me crazy. There was no organization in there, Damian. It was pure chaos," she says, and I can't contain my laughter.

"Fair enough. It was chaos," I say, placing the mop in the sink and picking up the towels from the floor. "Can you make it to the bathroom to get those shorts off? I'm going to toss these in the washer and bring you clean pants and underwear."

"I should be able to make it without too much of a mess," she says as she begins hobbling toward the half bath around the corner.

Going back to the closet, I find my phone on a shelf and bring up my sister's contact info. Starting the washer, I add soap and the dirty towels while I wait for her to answer.

"Joe's Pizza and Pub," she says upon answering.

"Her water broke."

"It's go time. I'll be there as soon as possible," she says and immediately hangs up the phone, leaving me to stare at my screen a moment before remembering I need to get clothes and bags and Avery into the car.

"How you doing?" I ask as I walk into the bathroom holding sweatpants, underwear, and a handful of maxi pads.

Elise looks up at me from the toilet and without missing a beat says, "Fantastic. Let's go have a baby."

Chapter 27

ELISE

All the books have said it could be hours and hours, even days. Everything says contractions will get closer together over time.

Lies. All of it. Every body is different. Every baby is different. Every new life is different.

And when I tell you this whole life has been a fucking ride, I'm putting it nicely. From my water breaking until this little guy came screaming into the world it was a grand total of one hour and forty-two minutes. Angela didn't make it to the hospital, none of our parents woke up to the phone calls, and Avery got to be in the room to watch her new baby brother be born.

But would I change how it's all happened to this point? Nope.

Arriving on April 11, three weeks before his due date, Maddox Lee Nowell joined our unconventional little family. Watching Damian become a father has been the greatest gift he could give me. I know throughout this entire adventure he's felt I'm the one giving him something, but I don't know if he realizes how much he's done for me and Avery by including us in his decision to be a dad.

"You should be sleeping," he says, quietly from the chair beside my bed.

His two days growth of beard makes him look older, but the tiny, dark-haired little prince sleeping in the crease of his right arm and the blonde-haired beauty tucked into his left side make him look like my perfect match.

"I can't. I would miss this too much," I say, laying my head on the pillow to watch him. "This is a really good look on you."

"You think so?" he asks, tipping his gaze to Maddox.

As if he knows his daddy has eyes on him, he shifts in his swaddle and lets out a quiet grunt.

"Hotter than you were twelve hours ago," I whisper, a small smile forming on my lips.

"What do you think about having another one as soon as possible?" he asks, winking.

"I think you're crazy and we're going to wait a bit. Enjoy the two we have first," I say, laughing softly. "Doesn't mean we can't practice a lot once I'm ready, though."

He looks at me thoughtfully, but I can't read the expression on his face. It's a mixture of adoration and exhilaration, but maybe like me it's just pure exhaustion.

"I love you, Elise. I've never been as happy as I am with you," he says. His eyes mist over and I can't help having the same reaction. "When I left my laptop open a year ago, I never would have expected to wind up here with you. Thank you for choosing me."

"We chose each other."

Epilogue

ONE YEAR LATER
DAMIAN

"So, here's the deal, okay? You're going to go out and tell Mom that Maddox and I need her help."

"What do I tell her you need help with? She's going to ask," Avery says. Her six-year-old brain works way too fast for me some days. "What if she's in the middle of hanging balloons and is standing on a chair? I don't want to scare her."

This kid is so full of imagination and love and creativity. I can't handle her some days. She comes home from school and if she doesn't have homework, she's in my office working on a new crazy idea or downstairs in the playroom. Sometimes I miss Little Avery who used to snuggle with me and watch movies, but I love watching her grow into the person she's meant to be.

"Don't worry, Sunshine, just tell her I need her help and you don't know what it is," I say, pulling the custom T-shirt over Maddox's head and slipping his arms in the fabric. Maybe I should rethink this. Before the party probably isn't the best time. "I know she's stressing out and I want her to see him in his outfit before everyone gets here. It's not really all that serious."

It's been a year full of change for us. Beginning with bringing the baby home and me having a crash course in newborn care. I know I would have figured it out if I was truly doing it on my own, but having Elise here with me made the transition so much easier. My respect for her as a single parent grew exponentially, despite already worshipping the ground she walks on.

"Your mama is going to think this outfit is the bomb," I say to Maddox. He smiles, showing off the two bottom teeth that finally came in a few weeks ago.

Elise going back to work after an extended leave because of summer break gave the two of us time to bond with the baby and each other. Then when summer arrived, Avery was able to spend more time with Maddox. It's not that she hadn't already bonded with him, because she was attached to him from the moment he was born, but after those first couple of months he was less of a "potato," as she called him, and more fun to play with.

It wasn't until recently that Avery finally started asking serious questions about Tanner. He calls occasionally, but is still in jail even after his attorney was able to argue his case down from second-degree aggravated assault to third-degree assault. He's supposed to be out in the next two years. The fact Avery caught on that he kept telling her he couldn't video chat with her prompted us to try to explain all the whys — why he can't come see her and why he's in jail. We could not answer her questions when she asked why he hurt someone instead of trying to talk to them, because we don't understand it any more than she does.

With so many things happening concurrently, I've been waiting. It feels like I've been waiting my whole life. I could have done this at any point in the last twelve months. All it would have taken is me pulling the box out of the safe and asking. I wanted to make sure it was fun and unconventional and special … just like us.

As I hear Avery running back down the hall, I pop the last button through the hole and smooth down Maddox's miniature jersey. The real surprise is his undershirt, but the main outfit was all Elise and Avery's idea — a baseball jersey with a number 1 on the back with our last name and on the front there's a golden eagle for the school Angela works at. The rest of us big kids have matching jerseys, also with last names and our ages. I wasn't opposed to the ages, but I might have put up a little fight about Avery and Elise having different names than me and Maddox. It might have been more than a little fight. There might be an Elise size jersey in our closet with her age and my last name on it because I wanted it on hand just in case I got up the nerve before today.

"She's coming!" Avery says bursting through the door.

"What's wrong?" Elise says coming in the bedroom hot on Avery's heels. "I was putting together the chicken dip. I might have spilled some. Your parents are on their way, my parents are on the way, Ang and Julia both just pulled in, I still need to shower and … what's wrong?"

Picking Maddox up off the changing table, I smile at the scene before me.

"Take a deep breath," I say, calmly walking over to her. I wrap my free arm around her and pull her close to me until her arms surround me and Maddox. Avery pushes in against us and completes our little circle.

"Everything is fine. Angela has the cake, Julia has whatever she was bringing, our parents will get here when they get here. Everyone else will show up on time."

"I know. I just want everything to be perfect," she says, touching her index finger to Maddox's nose.

He raises his arms and leans forward for Elise to take him, which she does willingly. All of the worries we had, the crazy ideas about whether or not she would love him, if we'd be upset if he didn't look like me, all of it — gone. While he definitely has some of the features from his egg donor, he is Elise's son through-and-through.

"Hi, my sweet boy. I still can't believe you've been here for an entire year. These shirts came out great. I'm so glad we went with the baseball theme. I can't wait to get pictures of us all together once he opens his T-ball set," she says against his hair. "Okay, back to Daddy. I need to get cleaned up while you go play with Aunt Ang and Daddy finishes the food."

Kissing Maddox on the temple and handing him back to me, Elise kisses me on the lips, nipping the bottom one gently. Then she leans down and kisses Avery on the head so as not to leave her out. Unable to keep my eyes off her, I watch as she rushes from the nursery and down the hall to our bedroom.

"Hey Angela," I say, walking into the kitchen a few minutes later. "Do you think this is too cliché?"

Pulling Maddox's jersey up enough for my sister to see the shirt beneath it, she snickers.

"I mean, it's not cliché, but it's not not cliché."

Looking at Maddox, I seriously consider changing him out of it and waiting until I can come up with something more clever.

"I know. I was really going for not, but not not will have to do. Right?" I sigh. "I can design entire buildings but apparently will absolutely mess this one thing up."

Julia reaches for Maddox and he eagerly goes to her. She immediately became another adopted aunt for the kids when Maddox was born, and her love for both Avery and Maddox help fill the void when my sister can't be around, though Angela makes sure she's home as often as possible.

"Hey, my guy! Your dad is worrying too much. Mama is going to love it," she says to the baby as he touches her face. Looking from Angela to Avery to me, she adds, "You are overthinking this. She's been waiting for this

193

moment for years and I really don't think there's any way you can mess it up unless you just don't do it at all."

"If you say so."

"We do," she says for both her and Angela. "Now go check on her and make sure she isn't freaking out about not having everything ready. Ang and I will finish up."

I take my leave and let my sister and Julia be in charge for the time being. It's something Elise and I have both had to come to terms with — giving up control when it's necessary — and Julia has been instrumental in helping Elise with that. I know my sister is her best friend from childhood, but Julia really has become family for us all.

As I enter our bedroom, the shower turns off and I momentarily freeze as if I'm not sure about knocking on the bathroom door or just entering. Then there's the fleeting thought that I should just sit on the bed and wait for her to come out. Shoving my hands in the pockets of my jeans, I touch the cold metal and loop the tip of my finger through it.

I could just do it right now and bypass the whole cute T-shirt thing, I think.

The ring has been in my pocket all morning. As soon as Elise got up, I took my shower and hid it in my jeans so I didn't have to scramble later in the day. And now here I am contemplating removing all the extras and just—

"You okay, Damian?" she asks, standing in the bathroom door in just her underwear and bra with her hair up in a towel.

"Perfect," I say, pulling my hands from my pockets.

She deserves all the extras.

Eyeing me suspiciously for a moment, Elise then nods and walks to the closet. She bends, releasing her hair from the towel, before grabbing a T-shirt and pulling it over her head. Slipping into a pair of snug fitting black jeans, she pulls a baseball jersey that matches Maddox's from a hanger and gracefully slides it on. As her fingers work the buttons into each hole, I cannot take my eyes off her. Something as simple as getting dressed should not be the turn on it is, but here we are.

"You're kind of freaking me out. You're sure everything is okay?"

"Yes, absolutely," I say, swallowing in an attempt to wet my throat. "We just don't have time to do all the things I'd like to do right now."

She laughs, walking back into the bathroom to hang her towel. I place myself strategically against the doorframe and watch in the mirror as she carefully applies eyeliner and lip gloss.

"And what would you like to do right now other than go celebrate our son's birthday?"

"If I tell you ... we're going to be late to the party and it's only in the living room," I say.

Her lips form an O and her eyes widen.

"I see," she responds, as her cheeks pink slightly when the understanding hits her.

"Maybe later. As long as you wear the jersey," I say, then push off the doorframe and walk away as I hear the first guest arrive.

*****

The entire day went as planned. As planned as we could have hoped for, anyway. Let's face it, we had a loosely designed schedule for cake and presents and the rest of it was toddlers from playgroup running around, falling down, and giggles. So many giggles.

As the day winds down and the last tiny friend leaves with their parents, only family remains. Julia, Angela, and Elise are in the kitchen putting leftovers away and dividing up the cake Ang bought from The Bakery on Main so a small portion stays at our house and the rest doesn't. We don't need that much cake here.

Walking into the room, I hand Maddox to Elise and let her know I'm going to go check on Avery.

"Sure. She should be in her room. She said she needed to change her shirt. Maybe you can convince her to not add more laundry to the already overflowing hamper?" she asks, as I kiss her on the temple.

"I'll do my best," I say. But, I walk away with every intention of letting her change her shirt.

I lightly knock on Avery's bedroom door and she pops it open. Looking up at me, she smiles and opens the door wide enough for me to come inside.

"Hurry up!" she scolds.

"Dang, I'm trying. There was cleanup and your brother was being a wiggle monster. You've got it on?"

She nods her head feverishly. When I went to Avery to tell her I was planning to ask — finally — she wanted to be part of everything. She has impressed me time and again with her ability to keep this secret.

"So, I'll go out to the kitchen and tell Mom you need her to get Maddox ready for a bath and to put his jersey in the laundry room because it has frosting on it," she says. "Then while she's doing that, you need to get the ring ready. Right?"

"Right."

Because if it goes how I think it will go, she won't bother taking him to his room to get him out of his clothes. Since he started eating solid food and making messes, she's gotten him mostly undressed in the kitchen or living room before taking him to the bath. Statistically, she'll do the same thing this time.

"Maddox has the shirt on?"

"Yes," I say, amused by her excitement.

"Then let's do this already!"

Avery runs from the bedroom, her light blue T-shirt plain on the front but on the back there's a message and if all goes as planned, Elise will read it after she sees Maddox's shirt.

"Mom!" I hear her yell. "D asked if you'd get Maddox ready for a bath. ... Just take his shirt off out here since it needs to go in the laundry. Damian said it has frosting on it and needs to be pretreated."

That's my cue and I walk out to the edge of the living room, watching as Elise lays the baby on the floor and begins unbuttoning his little jersey that matches the ones we're wearing. Angela, Julia, and all four parents gather in the wide doorway between the living room and kitchen as quietly as they can.

"You made such a mess, Bub, but that cake was so good. We're going to have to draw a picture and send a thank you to Delilah," Elise says as she continues unbuttoning the baby's jersey while he squirms on the floor. She leans down and blows raspberries on his belly and is greeted with big baby belly laughs.

When I see her reach the last button, I nod to Avery. She walks over and stands in front of Elise with her back to her mom as I pull the ring from my pocket and drop down on one knee, keenly aware that everything we're doing is on display. I have a fleeting, panicked thought, that she'll say no.

"I heard you like diamonds?" she reads out loud, quietly questioning, as she picks the baby up off the floor. "Damian?"

When she looks up in an effort to find me and sees Avery's back in front of her instead, she laughs when confronted with the image of a baseball diamond. The birthday party was baseball themed, so I took a chance, you know?

"After all, diamonds are a girl's best friend," she reads, her tone more questioning with each word added. "Um, okay."

She stands up, pulling Maddox's jersey off as she goes, and as she turns with the shirt in her hand she stops. It's me. I'm all she sees. Down on one knee and waiting as she holds her breath for a beat, making me second guess that she's ready for this step. My brain is screaming at me, asking why she hasn't said anything when I'm clearly asking her a very important question.

When she finally speaks, my cheeks heat and I can't help laughing at myself.

"You know ... you haven't actually asked me anything yet. I can't answer a question before it's asked. Communication is key to a healthy relationship."

"Always the devil's advocate, even now," I say, and she knows I'm referring to the last time I told her I wanted something and didn't come right out and ask her opinion on the matter. But the smile on her face is more important to me than being right. "Elise, will you marry me? I know we've done everything backwards, but you're the only one I want to move forward with for the rest of my life. Will you be my wife?"

Looking down at the baby on her hip and Avery standing beside her, she scrunches up her nose.

"Oh my god, Elise, just say yes already!" Angela yells from the door. "This is the birth certificate argument all over again. I can't stand it. Just be my sister-in-law already!"

We both turn to look at my sister who is practically vibrating with excitement, but Julia quickly clamps a hand over Angela's mouth as Elise turns her attention back to the kids.

"What do you two think? Should we give him a chance? He's been a pretty awesome dad so far," she says, and it's killing me. "Do you think he'll make a good husband?"

"He's been the best dad," Avery says, looking up at her mother. Hands on her hips, she stands tall and her eyes find mine. Taking a big breath in and letting it out dramatically, she says, "Yeah, I think we should keep him."

"That's a pretty fair assessment," Elise says, catching my eye as her smile begins to form.

"So, is that a 'yes?' Will you choose me?"

Through laughter, that turns to tears, Elise finally says, "Yes."

"I will choose you forever."

Acknowledgements

I am not a fast writer, so when I say this book came out of me quickly it's no lie. Despite the kids being out of school for the summer when I started writing Damian and Elise's story, I didn't fall behind. That in itself is a small miracle. I began writing two weeks before *The Bakery on Main* was released in June and somehow finished my initial draft in five months (plus 10 days, but who's counting, right?). Editing and the draft for beta readers was done four weeks after that and I started writing another book before Christmas 2024.

The reality is, I also didn't talk about this book much with anyone. I kept it under wraps because there were a lot of other things happening. I was trying to spend as much time as possible writing the book instead of talking about the book. But, there were a few of you who found your way into my orbit:

Coffee and sourdough toast: Stay classy. Thanks for helping me power through those rough mornings.

Spotify: Never take away the "enable repeat one" feature. Some songs just hit differently with certain scenes and I have to listen to them 15,690,332 times in a row. Okay? Cool.

Carrie and Vicci: You are both so amazing. Your feedback is always thoughtful and I cannot begin to express how much it means to have your support as friends and readers. I'm indebted to you both and eternally grateful the book world has brought us together.

Vicci (again) and Laura: Thank you for listening to me whine and helping me talk through some of the issues I had with this book while we were at RomantiConn and DelaConn. I was definitely struggling at times. First round of margaritas are on me at the next event.

Allisyn: From the check ins to the advice when I was freaking out about this project, I am so glad we connected.

Ron and Sean: I am so fortunate to have dudes in my life who read romance. The fact I don't even have to ask if you want to read the next book, but rather when would you like the link, should scare me a little but it just makes me feel secure in our relationship and friendship, respectively. I really lucked out in 2003.

Boy: I will never be sorry to see you cry while reading one of my books. Your ability to show emotion and be vulnerable is one of the many things I admire about you. You're a partner who loves with your whole heart. You're a dad who shows up. You're my favorite book boyfriend. I will choose you forever.

About the Author

M.L. Pennock is a former journalist turned author. She attended Alfred University, earning a Bachelor of Arts in English and communication studies, before going on to earn a Master of Arts in communications from SUNY College at Brockport. She lives in Central New York with her husband, four children, and Siberian Husky, Tikaani.

M.L. Pennock is the author of the To Have series and a spinoff series, Famous in a Small Town.

Visit facebook.com/mlpennock or mlpennock.com for more information about what she's working on next.

www.ingramcontent.com/pod-product-compliance
Lightning Source LLC
Chambersburg PA
CBHW051251250626
47155CB00009B/3249

* 9 7 8 1 7 3 2 7 8 1 7 3 3 *